DARKNESS IN TIBER

THE SOUL BOUND SAGA
BOOK TWO

JAMES E WISHER

SAND HILL PUBLISHING

Edited by: Janie Linn Dullard

Cover art by: B-Ro

ISBN: 978-1-68520-027-5

010120231.0

CHAPTER 1

J oran Den Cade sat beside Mia on the passenger couch on the bridge of an imperial dragon ship. The massive flying ship hung beneath an even bigger balloon filled with a lighter-than-air alchemical gas. A bridge crew of four oversaw the ship's operation. The captain and another fellow he'd come to think of as the assistant captain shouted orders to the rest of the crew via speaking tubes that jutted up through the floor. A stern woman that served as the ship's navigator sat at a bolted-down desk covered with maps and other cartography supplies. And finally a spotter stood looking down through an ultra-hard glass viewport that pointed straight down.

Today the crew all looked especially nervous. The cause of their nervousness being the pacing figure of the Iron Princess, Alexandra Tiberius. Her sandals slapped against the hull as she made her next pass, a deep frown creasing her lovely features. Though only a few years older than Joran, Alexandra commanded the entire imperial army. No one would have guessed the mind of a tactical genius resided in such a beautiful woman. That was just one of her many advantages.

1

Only Joran and his soulmate, Mia, knew the reason for her agitation. After finally bringing peace to the restive province of Stello, a messenger had arrived from the capital to tell her that her father, the emperor, lay dying. This seemed impossible to Joran as the emperor had access to the finest healers and alchemists in the empire. Nothing save old age or sudden violence should have ended his rule and at barely over fifty, Marcus Tiberius still had many years left.

It was a mystery, one of many the Iron Princess, and by extension her personal advisor, Joran, had to solve.

"Tiber City is in sight," the assistant captain said.

Joran blew out a breath. Home at last. He'd worried that Alexandra's endless pacing would wear a hole in the deck. At least the ship hadn't exploded partway back, unlike her trip out from the capital.

"I've never seen her this anxious," Mia whispered in his ear.

Joran reached over and squeezed Mia's hand. Warmth and trust flowed through the soul bond that connected them. They shared a soul and no more powerful bond existed. Joran would do anything for Mia and she would do anything for him.

Though not classically beautiful like the princess, his soulmate had the lean, strong figure of a warrior along with the dark hair and bronze skin of an imperial. She'd also believed for a time that she loved Alexandra. And though she'd had that fantasy shattered, Joran knew Mia still lusted after the princess. No doubt along with many others that wanted either her power or body or, most likely, both. For his part, Joran wanted only a return to his peaceful life of research.

Not that he saw any path for that wish coming true. And even if he did, given the current state of the empire, he had an obligation as an imperial nobleman to do everything possible to help set things right.

Alexandra stalked up to the viewing window. "Finally! I thought we'd never get here."

Joran considered trying to reassure her, but doubted anything he might say would help. When your father lay dying, even well-intentioned words sounded trite. Still, if she wished, he would do his best as a master healer to try and help the emperor. Though what he could do that the palace healers couldn't, Joran had no clue.

Soon enough the sprawling city of Tiber filled the viewing window to such an extent that Joran saw it even from his position. The walled city consisted of three concentric circles. The outermost and largest housed the bulk of the city's population as well as the many markets and businesses. Craftsmen, modestly successful merchants, and lesser nobles lived in the second circle. And in the final circle sat the imperial palace along with the homes of the richest and most powerful families as well as the imperial college and the First Church of The One God.

Joran's home, Den Cade Manor, took up an above-average chunk of that neighborhood. Had he wished it, Joran likely could have seen it from the ship. He did not at all wish to see it. He preferred to pretend they weren't several thousand feet in the air.

The dragon ship began to descend and Alexandra stalked toward the rear of the bridge where the exit waited. Joran and Mia fell in behind her followed by her personal protectors, the Iron Guard.

"After I speak to my brother, you will check on Father," Alexandra said in a tone that brooked no argument.

"As you wish, Majesty," Joran said. "I won't be stepping on any toes, will I?"

"I don't care if you break every foot in the palace. I trust no one else to tell me what's really going on with my father. After everything that's happened, you're the only one I have complete faith in."

Joran kept his expression carefully neutral. He had great

confidence in his abilities, but Joran was still only twenty-two. Many alchemists with vastly greater experience would no doubt consider his elevation to Alexandra's personal advisor ill-considered at best and absolute stupidity at worst. He knew plenty of the people that would voice those opinions. They were the same people that said he didn't deserve to be made a grand-master despite fulfilling all the requirements.

He'd just have to show them all how wrong they were.

They reached the lowest level of the dragon ship and a moment later a slight lurch indicated that they'd landed. As the boarding ramp lowered, the messenger that brought the news about the emperor's condition came rushing to join them. To his visible annoyance, Alexandra led the way down.

Joran took a deep breath and smiled. No exotic perfume filled the air and the blistering heat had vanished. Summer would soon be gone and real autumn would arrive. Even under the circumstances, his pleasure at being home nearly over-whelmed him.

"This is the happiest you've been since we met," Mia said.

"It's as much relief as happiness, but yes, I'm glad to be home."

Having grown up basically in the shadow of the palace, the sight of it didn't overawe him the way it might some. The airfield covered a large section of the eastern quarter of the palace grounds. In addition to their dragon ship, two more floated a little ways away. One had the imperial eagle painted on the side of the balloon. It looked nearly as big as the serpent he'd helped kill.

The palace itself loomed in the distance. It sprawled over a hundred acres with wings, gardens, connecting walkways, and everything else imaginable. He'd never actually visited the place, but Mother said she did once years ago. She considered it a highlight of her life.

Alexandra had no interest in any of the sights. She made straight for the waiting carriage, a crimson and gold monstrosity pulled by four white horses. A footman in matching livery hastened to open the door for her.

"Where's my brother?" Alexandra asked.

"His Imperial Highness is with your father. Word has already been sent to the palace. I'm sure you'll wish to clean up and change."

Alexandra looked like she'd enjoy little more than strangling the snooty little man, but she only nodded and climbed aboard. Joran and Mia joined her, drawing disapproving looks from the footman.

When they'd settled in a whip cracked and the carriage lurched into motion.

"He seemed a bit full of himself for a servant," Joran said.

"Oh, they're all like that," Alexandra said. "The palace runs on a mix of arrogance and formality. The One God forbid a member of the family doesn't wear the right outfit or say the right thing. That's why I prefer being in the field with the army. Marcus seems to thrive on it, bless him."

"Where does that leave us, Majesty?" Mia asked.

"As my advisor, Joran will stay in my suite and go where I go. As his bodyguard, you will stay with him. You'll need new robes and I assume you have your amulet."

Joran pulled the platinum amulet out of his tunic and let it rest on his chest.

"Good. Mia, you can wear your uniform. As a commoner, no one expects you to dress like a noble." Alexandra didn't say it like an insult, but Joran felt Mia's internal wince all the same.

He glanced out the window at the groundskeepers fussing with flower beds and topiary. They might have been slaves or servants. Joran couldn't tell for sure at this distance.

At last they stopped in front of the palace. Not at the main entrance as he expected, but in front of one of the smaller doors. The snooty footman opened the carriage door for them again and Alexandra crunched her way across the white gravel to the door. She raised an eyebrow at the footman, who hastened to open that one as well. He remained outside, closing the door behind Mia.

A short, whitewashed hall led to a sitting room bigger than the entire suite they'd used in Cularo. Five beautiful female servants in white tunics that left their legs bare from midthigh down stood silently along the wall. They might have been related to the Cularo servants with their dark hair and bronze skin.

When Alexandra entered the room, they hurried forward and bowed. "Welcome home, Majesty," they said in unison.

"I have a meeting with my brother soon. Prepare a bath." Alexandra pointed at Joran and Mia. "This is my personal advisor, Joran Den Cade. He and his soulmate will be staying in the guest quarters. Consider an order from him, an order from me. Joran, do whatever you need to before the examination. You'll begin as soon as Marcus and I finish talking."

Joran bowed. "As you command, Majesty."

Alexandra strode off with four of the servants fluttering along behind her. The fifth led Joran to a suite of rooms big enough to comfortably house a family of six. He eyed the big feather bed but didn't dare get too comfortable. He contented himself with setting his kit beside one of the overstuffed leather chairs and sitting.

"Would you care for refreshment, my lord?" the servant asked.

"I could eat. Mia?"

"Me too." She dropped into a second chair across a coffee table from him.

"Whatever you have handy would be wonderful, along with wine," Joran said.

The servant bobbed a curtsy and hurried out.

"You feel tense," Mia said. "What happened to relief at being home?"

"Oh, I'm still relieved. It's just that soon the next battle begins and this is one I'm not sure you can fight for me."

CHAPTER 2

Some people had homes; Alexandra had a place where she lived. Not that she would ever complain about living in the palace with servants eager to obey her every whim, all the food she wanted, and a small army to keep her safe. Having seen plenty of the empire, she understood exactly how good she'd had it from the time she was a kid. Still, it wasn't your typical family life, especially since Mother died when she was two. The servants raised her for the most part. Father always had court duties.

She smiled as she strode down the empty hall toward the family's private garden, her hard-soled sandals clacking against the stone floor. She felt naked without her sword and guards. Even knowing no safer place existed, thoughts of assassins and sabotage constantly flitted through her mind. She'd have trouble escaping in the elaborately wrapped purple robes the servants had dressed her in. The stiletto she hid in a sheath on her thigh offered her some comfort, however.

Forcing the dark thoughts away, she focused on the garden and her upcoming reunion with Marcus. The garden was the one place the servants avoided, at least when a member of the family visited. Here, even Father had a chance to pretend he didn't rule an empire of millions, all of whom looked to him for their safety and wellbeing. Some of her happiest memories happened here.

As soon as she opened the door, the tinkle of the fountain mingling with the smell of fall flowers brought her right back to being a little girl.

"Hello, sister."

The servants would call her pace unseemly as she practically ran to the white marble gazebo in the center of the garden. Marcus stood at her approach and they hugged. It felt so good to be just brother and sister for a moment.

She stepped back to look at him and her smile withered. Marcus looked worn out. He had dark circles under his bloodshot eyes. His usually glowing bronze skin had a sallow tint and his face looked sunken and hollow. If she didn't know he turned thirty-two several months ago, Alexandra would have guessed he was older than Father.

"You look horrible and I'm the one that's been fighting a war."

He scrubbed a hand across his face and they sat side by side in the cushioned chairs. "I've been carrying out all of Father's duties while pretending he isn't that sick. Everyone knows I'm lying. I get these subtle questions about why Father hasn't taken a cure all. I keep saying he isn't sick enough to need one, that he just needs rest. But he keeps getting worse."

"Why don't you tell me everything from the beginning. When I left for Cularo, Father seemed fine."

"He was," Marcus said. "Then two days later he got a cough. Cordius listened to his chest and suggested a cure all just in case. Father took it that night expecting to be all better in the morning. When the servants came to help him dress, he was so weak he couldn't get out of bed. Cordius didn't know what had happened and prepared a second cure all. It did no good. Father has taken one every morning since. The healer says that's all that's keeping him alive."

"Cordius has been the family healer since before we were born. Do you think he's gotten too old to do the job?"

Marcus shook his head. "He seems sharp as a razor. I fear whatever's wrong with Father is simply beyond healing."

His voice cracked and Marcus broke into sobs. "I'm not ready for this. I can't be emperor. I'm not strong like you and Father."

Alexandra held him as he cried. Her brother had always been the sensitive one in the family. Not exactly ideal for the future ruler of the empire.

When he finally got himself under control Marcus wiped his face and said, "You'll stay, won't you? If we're together it won't be so bad. At least until everyone accepts that I'm in command."

"Of course I'll stay, but if you don't mind, I'd like to have my advisor take a look at Father. Joran has saved my life twice and proven highly competent as both a healer and alchemist. I don't wish to say anything bad about Cordius, but a second set of eyes might see something he missed."

"You trust this man?"

"With my life. We wouldn't even have Stello Province if not for him."

Marcus's smile returned. "You'll have to tell me everything about this fellow. He must be something to earn the trust of the Iron Princess."

"Don't start. When can Joran see him?"

"Right now. Collect your friend and we'll meet at Father's bedchamber."

Joran and Mia followed Alexandra through the palace toward the emperor's bedchamber. The halls were immaculate, decorated in gold with crimson tapestries. Alchemical lights glowed every ten paces and their strides made no sound as they stepped on thick carpet. He seriously doubted anyone as low-ranking as him, and certainly not Mia, had ever set foot in this part of the palace before.

Soon enough they started passing soldiers dressed in the imperial colors with golden eagles on their chests. The emperor's personal guards were said to be the finest and most loyal fighters in the empire. Nevertheless, he feared some infiltrator may have found a way to join their ranks, unlikely as it seemed. Alexandra ordering Mia to leave her sword behind did nothing to calm him.

"Walk me through it again, please," Joran said, as much to take his mind off his suspicions as because he actually needed a refresher. "The healer gave him a cure all for a simple cough?"

"Out of an abundance of caution, or so Marcus said." She glanced back at him. "Giving a cure all to someone not really sick wouldn't do anything to them, right?"

"No. It would simply guarantee an excellent night's sleep as well as a morning free of aches or pains. One of your many-times-great grandfathers took a cure all once a week as a precaution." Joran scratched his chin. He'd never treated someone as important as the emperor, but in his experience, no healer liked to use a cure all unless everything else had failed, an occasional historical anomaly aside. "Will His Imperial Majesty's personal healer be joining us for this examination?"

"Cordius knows nothing about it. Since we're basically questioning his competence, we deemed it wise to say nothing until after."

"Forgive my saying so, but that seems more thoughtful than usual."

"The imperial family, including my brother and his family, rely on Cordius to keep them healthy. If we can't trust him, there's no point in him serving in his current position. My request and Marcus's desperation are the only reason you're getting this chance."

They reached a set of double doors inlaid with a huge imperial eagle and guarded by a squad of ten men. The guards all saluted fist to heart and one of them pushed the doors open.

Mia hadn't said a word since they left Alexandra's suite and her anxiety only grew as the group stepped into the emperor's bedchamber. The huge room was bigger than Joran's apartment. It held a bed big enough for ten, dressers, mirrors, tables, wardrobes, and anything else you might think of. On the left side of the bed, nestled amid the covers, lay the emperor. A younger version of the man stood at his bedside. The exhausted-looking fellow had to be Alexandra's brother and the heir to the throne.

Joran swallowed, but let none of the tension he felt at being in a room with three of the most powerful people in the empire show. His phony noble mask firmly in place, Joran bowed. "Your Imperial Highness."

Marcus forced his gaze away from his unconscious father and Joran saw his red, tired eyes for the first time. He'd clearly been crying and not long ago. Hopefully he reserved such a show of weakness for private moments. If any of the high-ranking nobles saw him like this, they'd swallow him whole, heir to the throne or not.

A faint, humorless smile creased Marcus's face. "You will be Joran Den Cade. Alexandra speaks highly of your abilities. I swear to you in my father's name that if you can find some way to cure him, anything that you desire will be yours."

That promise from this man meant almost literally what he said. With the empire's power, he could offer Joran just about anything. Happily for everyone, Joran wanted nothing more than a safe and prosperous empire that assured he'd be well rewarded for his skills. That in turn would assure his family's future.

"I will do my best. With your permission, I'll begin my examination. Mia, will you help me, please?"

"Me?" Her voice came out as a high squeak.

"Your enhanced senses may detect something I miss. And at some point, I may need an extra pair of hands. I trust none more than yours."

"Okay, just tell me what to do."

He gave her hand a squeeze and set his kit on the floor beside the bed. Since the problem started in the emperor's lungs, he'd begin there. He took an item that resembled a trumpet from his kit, placed the wide end on the emperor's chest and the narrow end to his ear.

Joran held his breath and listened. The heart sounded strong, but the lungs held a faint wheeze. Not enough to worry him under other circumstances, but worth noting now.

He backed away and motioned Mia over. "I heard only a wheeze. See if you hear anything else."

"Like what?"

"A rattle, a catch, anything at all out of the ordinary."

She put her ear to the listening tube, face scrunched in concentration. After a few seconds she said, "No, I only hear the wheeze. Is that good?"

"Better than the alternatives. Put your face next to his and when I press on his chest take a deep sniff. Focus on signs of decay—"

Marcus let out a groan.

Joran glanced at Alexandra. She went to her brother and tried to soothe him.

He put the pair out of his mind and asked, "Ready?"

Mia moved so close to the emperor it looked like she

planned to kiss him and nodded. Joran pressed lightly on his chest and a puff of air rushed out.

"There's something, not like rot though. More like…I don't know. It's vaguely familiar, but I can't put my finger on it."

"Switch with me."

This time Mia pressed and Joran sniffed. He recognized the problem at once. Before he could speak, the bedroom doors burst open and an old man dressed in flowing crimson robes with a snowy beard strode in.

He glared around the room, seeming totally unintimidated by the gathered imperial family. "Why are amateurs pawing at my patient? The emperor needs rest, not the touch of strangers."

As far as Joran could tell, the emperor didn't even know they were here. Not wanting to upset anyone, he kept that observation to himself. Best to stay silent and let Alexandra handle this.

"Since when does the imperial family answer to you, Cordius?" Alexandra asked. "Joran is a fully qualified and competent healer. I asked him to offer a second opinion on what's ailing Father and the last I checked, I didn't need your permission to do so."

That meshed with Joran's thinking, but he still kept silent. Much as he'd like to confirm his assumption and try to see how long the emperor had left, he felt confident he'd found the problem.

Cordius turned to Marcus. "You went along with this folly, Highness? Don't you trust me to tend your father?"

Marcus patted the air, trying to calm the old man. "Of course I trust you. Your service to the family has been exemplary for decades. But under the current circumstances, a second set of eyes seemed prudent. Alexandra, perhaps we should continue this later."

"Perhaps I should resign as imperial healer!" Cordius said. "I'll not be second-guessed by some pup!"

Mia's anger hit him and she took a step toward Cordius.

Joran caught her wrist and shook his head. "I beg your pardon, sir. Her Majesty wished me to examine her father. I did so confident that a man of your experience wouldn't miss anything where your patients were concerned. Forgive me if I disturbed His Imperial Majesty in any way."

That little speech seemed to calm the old man, who took a deep breath. "No, forgive me, young man. I've been so frustrated at my inability to heal the emperor that I fear I've let my anger get the better of me."

Joran bowed. "Thank you for your understanding, sir. Majesty, shall we withdraw?"

"Very well. Marcus, we'll speak later." Alexandra stalked off. Joran collected his kit and hurried to follow, pulling Mia along behind him.

No one said anything until they reached Alexandra's suite and the servants had been dismissed.

"Why did you let him speak to you like that?" Mia asked. "You're twice the alchemist he is. At least!"

Alexandra settled into a chair and pointed at the couch. Joran and Mia sat side by side, facing her. "You were very deferential. I brought you to my father's side to hear your opinion, not watch you play up to Cordius. I trust you have an explanation."

"I didn't want him to do anything rash."

Alexandra blinked. "I don't believe Cordius has done anything rash in fifty years. What, exactly, did you fear he might do?"

"Kill your father."

Alexandra leapt to her feet. "What?!"

The servants appeared from the room they shared in the rear of the suite. "Is all well, Majesty?" one of them asked.

She shot them a glare hot enough to strip paint. "If I see your faces again before I summon you, I'll see you sold to the cheapest whorehouse in Oceanus Province."

The young ladies fled back the way they'd come. The shouting at least seemed to calm Alexandra.

"Why did you fear Cordius might kill my father?"

"Because he's been doing it in slow motion for some time. I'm not entirely certain how, but I smelled poison on your father's breath when Mia pressed on his chest. It's Black Bile of the Earth. How he's diluting it enough to keep the emperor from instantly dying, I'm not certain."

"You're sure?" Alexandra asked. "There's no doubt in your mind?"

"None." Joran would never mistake the stink of Black Bile, especially after smelling it so recently. "I also have no proof."

Alexandra sat back down. "That's a problem. Marcus trusts the old man absolutely. I doubt I could even convince him to allow a search of Cordius's workshop. There is another option, but I'll have to share a secret known only to the imperial family."

"Considering the number of secrets we already share, does one more really matter?"

Alexandra smiled. "I suppose not. There are passages running through the palace walls. They're supposed to allow us to flee should the worst ever happen and Tiber falls. There are spy ports along the way so you can look into every room save mine, Marcus's, and Father's."

"What time does Cordius bring your father his cure all? I'll need to be in place at least an hour before then."

"I don't know," Alexandra said, her voice grim. "But I will find out."

CHAPTER 3

Joran stifled a yawn. It seemed Cordius brought the cure all to the emperor first thing in the morning, even before the crown prince rose for the day. A wise decision on his part. The fewer people he met, the less likely that someone might detect the scent of Black Bile. Not that Joran imagined anyone else noting the presence of such a small amount even if they knew what the poison smelled like.

Mia leaned on the wall beside him, gaze focused on the eye-sized peephole. She reminded him of a lioness on the hunt, ready to spring into motion at a moment's notice. He appreciated her presence more than he knew how to say. Joran felt certain he had strength enough to deal with a seventy-year-old man if he had to, but having someone that specialized in violence made him feel better.

The two of them had entered the narrow passage before dawn and made their way to their current location in the wall of Cordius's workshop. And what a workshop. Despite knowing what Cordius had done, Joran still marveled at the collection of equipment and supplies collected in the perfectly organized room. He considered his own lab at the college above average, but this made him drool.

He shook it off and focused as the man himself arrived. Mia immediately leaned back but didn't make a sound. Joran pressed his right eye to the opening so he wouldn't miss a detail. Their cheeks were practically touching.

Cordius got straight to work, lighting a small burner and putting the troll's blood on to heat. He followed the proper procedures, not varying in the slightest, until he set the completed cure all in a stand to cool. Next he went to a blank section of wall and touched a particular place. The wall slid down out of sight revealing a niche with a small, cylindrical flask made of metal.

That had to be it.

Joran eased back to let Mia see as well. Together they watched Cordius carry the flask over, cover his face with a mask identical to the one Joran wore when he extracted the Black Bile, and select a metal prod from the workbench. He dipped it in the flask and came up with a single drop that he let fall into the cure all. The potion darkened just a fraction, certainly not enough that anyone untrained would notice the difference.

They needed to tell Alexandra, right now.

Joran closed the spy hole and motioned Mia back the way they'd come. They tiptoed for twenty paces before breaking into a run. It took only a minute to reach Alexandra's suite. He pushed the door open and stepped out into the sitting room. The princess stood, arms crossed and toe tapping. She'd already changed into fine if more practical crimson robes and she wore her sword belted at her waist.

"Well?" she demanded before Joran even had a chance to close the door.

"I was right. He put a single drop of the poison into the cure all. That's why your father isn't improving. The Black Bile is negating the cure all even as the cure all negates the poison's lethal effects. It's a delicate balance. Cordius, or someone at least, must have killed dozens of people to find the right proportion. And the cost in reagents for those experiments boggles my mind. There are so many ways the palace healer might have killed the emperor without anyone knowing, I can't imagine why he chose such a long, convoluted path."

"We can ask him when he's strapped to the rack, but not until I put out both his eyes with hot pokers. Come on."

Alexandra marched out with Joran and Mia on her heels. This could go so badly in so many ways Joran didn't even want to think about it. He prayed to The One God that Alexandra kept her head. The imperial guards wouldn't attack her, at least he didn't think so, but if her brother showed up and didn't believe them, she might end up restrained.

Should that happen, Joran didn't know what he'd do. As heir to the throne, Marcus outranked Alexandra and for Joran to disobey him, even at her order and to save the emperor, might well see him executed and his family stripped of their wealth and standing. This was why he hated dealing with the nobility. So many ranks and you always had to know who you had to obey, who you were free to ignore, and who you could boss around.

The trio reached the emperor's bedchamber door just as the crown prince came around the corner from the opposite direction. He didn't look much better than he had during their first meeting. The poor man clearly hadn't slept more than a few hours last night.

Marcus brightened at the sight of his sister then frowned as his gaze shifted to the sword at her waist. "Alexandra, this is a surprise. I hadn't expected to see you until lunch this afternoon. What brings you here and why are you armed?"

She had no chance to answer before Cordius came down the hall, the poisoned cure all in his hand.

Alexandra leveled her sword at him and said, "I'm here because this disloyal swine has poisoned Father's cure all with Black Bile of the Earth."

Cordius stared at the tip of Alexandra's sword as if no one had ever pointed one at him. The shock lasted only a second. "What madness is this? My cure alls are the only things keeping your father alive. If you'll excuse me, Princess, I have to treat my patient."

Alexandra didn't flinch. "You will not give that cursed potion to my father. Should you take another step, much as I wish to know why you've betrayed my family's trust, I will separate your head from your shoulders."

"Will someone please tell me what's going on?" Marcus asked.

"What's going on, Your Imperial Highness, is I came to give your father his daily treatment and found your sister and her—" he made a disgusted wave at Joran and Mia "—entourage waiting. The next thing I know I'm being held at sword point while the emperor suffers without his medicine."

"Why don't you tell him about the poison you put in it so the cure all won't work? Joran figured it out yesterday. Whatever game you've been playing, it's over."

She clearly didn't want it known that Joran had used the secret passages. That would make explaining trickier if not downright impossible.

Cordius snorted. "Let me guess, he smelled something on the emperor's breath that resembled Black Bile of the Earth. It's a simple mistake for an inexperienced healer to make. I believe His Imperial Majesty has an alchemy-resistant fungus in his lungs and that's why the cure all isn't working. The smell is very similar to that evil poison. There's no shame in making such an error. A couple more decades of study and you'll know the difference as well. Now, if I can get on with my work?"

Marcus moved closer to the princess who showed no sign of

moving aside. "I know you have great faith in your new advisor, but surely of the two, Cordius is the one most likely to be correct. Perhaps you should stand down and let him give Father his treatment."

Alexandra turned to look at her brother, leaned in, and whispered something in his ear.

Marcus's jaw dropped a fraction. "You didn't."

"It was the only way to find out for sure. Can we take him into custody now?"

Marcus turned a hard, angry glare on Cordius. For the first time, Joran could actually picture him as emperor. "Guards, seize Cordius and take him to the dungeon."

"Strip him as well," Joran said before he thought better of it. "He may have some nasty surprises hidden in his robe."

"Oh, I have." Cordius raised his free hand, a vial clutched in it.

Everyone moved to stop him, but Mia moved fastest.

Cordius hurled the vial toward the floor.

She dove, arm extended, and caught it six inches above the stone.

The imperial guards rushed at Cordius.

The old healer backpedaled as he groped at his robe.

The nearest guard reached him half a stride too late.

Another vial shattered and a black mist filled the air.

Propriety be damned, Joran and Mia hustled the prince and princess back toward the emperor's bedchamber door. Luckily the mist dispersed well before it reached them. But not before it killed all ten guards. Of Cordius, no sign remained.

"We have to catch him," Marcus said. "I'll have that bastard's guts pulled out an inch at a time."

While the prince ranted, Mia handed Joran the vial she caught. "What is it?"

Joran held it up to the light and shook his head. "Can't tell by the color. Something unpleasant, no doubt."

He slipped it into his pocket for later study. "Majesty."

Alexandra turned away from her brother. "What?"

"Cordius didn't lie about one thing. The emperor needs a cure all before the accumulated Black Bile lingering in his body finishes him off. With your permission, I'll begin preparing a dose at once."

"You can use Cordius's lab," Marcus said.

"No, Your Imperial Highness, I wouldn't want to risk the possibility that he tainted his equipment in some way just in case this very thing happened. I have everything I need in my kit and can prepare the cure all in your father's chamber. If you wish my advice on one more matter, make sure you stop Cordius before he reaches his lab. He still has Black Bile and if he gets it in the palace cistern it could kill hundreds. The One God forbid he gets it in the city water supply."

Alexandra and Marcus shared a look before she sprinted away, sword still bare in her hands. "Guards! To the healer's lab with all haste!"

Marcus opened the door and ushered Joran in. "Do what you must."

Joran went to a table with a white marble top and got to work. By the time he finished, an hour later, the emperor had begun thrashing and moaning as the effects of his last treatment wore off.

"You'll need to hold him still," Joran said.

Marcus got out of his chair and went to the bed. He took a firm grip on his father's shoulders, but the emperor still squirmed too much to risk the cure all.

Marcus looked at Mia. "Help me."

The blood drained from her face, but Mia laid her hands on the emperor and held him steady. Joran quickly poured the potion into his open mouth. When he'd drained the vial they all moved back and watched, with bated breath.

Thirty seconds felt like thirty minutes, but the emperor finally let out a long sigh and settled into a deep, healing sleep.

"He hasn't looked this at ease in weeks." Marcus dropped back into his chair. "Please, let this be what heals him."

"I didn't dare give him the quick version, so he'll be asleep for at least three days." Joran finished packing his kit. "When he wakes, he'll be hungry. I recommend starting him off with broth and soaked bread. His strength should return quickly once the poison is purged. Perhaps a week for full recovery."

"The One God bless you, Joran Den Cade. I see now why my sister puts her faith in you. From this day forward, you have my permission to call me Marcus. When he wakes, I will tell Father all you've done for him. I'm sure he will reward you as I promised."

"Thank you, Marcus."

"We should go check on Her Majesty," Mia said.

Joran could have hugged her for giving him an excuse to leave. He bowed to Marcus. "If you'll excuse us?"

Marcus waved them off and Mia led the way out into the hall. A fresh group of guards had taken up positions outside the bedroom. Further up the hall, three bodies remained on the floor.

One of the new guards caught Joran's eye. "Her Majesty said you were to meet her at Cordius's lab as soon as you emerged."

Joran nodded. "Thanks."

When they'd rounded the bend out of sight Mia asked, "What does it mean that both the crown prince and the princess want you to call them by their first names?"

"Let me put it this way. If politics was quicksand, I'd be in it up to my neck and sinking fast." Any hope of a return to a normal life ended when he saved the emperor's life. Now he needed to figure out exactly what his new life would look like and how he'd survive.

———

Cordius huddled in an unused bedroom and gasped for breath. A man shouldn't have to run for his life after turning seventy. He also shouldn't be forced to perform a slow-motion assassination, but here he was. To say this had been a difficult month would be putting it mildly. Now he needed to escape the palace. No doubt the death the imperial siblings had planned for him didn't bear consideration.

Much as he'd like to stop at his lab, Cordius wasn't fool enough to walk right into the one place his hunters would seek him first. Unfortunately, that severely limited his options for escape. A few more nasty tricks hid in his robe and he'd use any of them without hesitation if he had to.

For the rest of his certainly short life, he'd curse the name Joran Den Cade. He'd hoped to intimidate or at least brush off the young man's observations, regardless of how accurate they were, but whatever the princess told her brother had convinced him that Cordius had deceived him. Everything had depended on the imperial family's trust. Once he lost that, the game ended.

His racing heart had slowed enough that he felt like moving again. A single step brought him to the door and he froze. Footsteps and raised voices outside said that the search had begun. His jaw clenched. More time, he needed more time, but how to buy it?

Since he had no intention of ever returning to the palace, he had one easy option. He pulled a vial of alchemist's fire from a hidden pocket, steeled himself, and stepped out into the hall.

The guards stared at him.

That moment of surprise gave him all he needed. Cordius hurled the vial at the nearest man and ran the opposite way.

The explosion seared his back.

He ignored the pain, running for all his aged body was

worth. A servant's exit lay not far away. Reaching the grounds guaranteed nothing, but it gave him the best chance to escape.

By some miracle he reached the nondescript door and found it unguarded.

Cordius slipped out into the fresh air.

As soon as he did, something heavy hit him, driving him to the ground. Powerful hands grabbed both his arms and forced them behind his back. Manacles bit into his wrists and someone hauled him to his feet.

Four guards surrounded him, all looking very pleased with themselves. "Bet we get a bonus for this," one of them said.

Another, older, man drew a shining dagger of imperial steel. "Orders are we strip him just in case he has any more surprises. Best hold still, traitor. I'd hate to cut your throat by mistake."

He didn't sound at all like he'd hate that and Cordius stayed still as a statue. The three remaining guards laughed and joked, paying not the least attention.

That ended up being their downfall.

The older guard lashed out, cutting and stabbing until all three lay dead at his feet. He cleaned the dagger, sheathed it, and removed Cordius's manacles.

Cordius hadn't said a word through the whole thing, his mind frozen by the sudden violence.

The guard grabbed him by the arm and dragged him toward the nearby barracks. "Our mutual friend isn't going to be pleased by your failure."

"Did the overseer send you to keep an eye on me?" Cordius asked.

"Not specifically, but given my position in the palace guard, it made sense that I'd be on the lookout for any betrayal."

"Please, I betrayed no one. That whelp Joran Den Cade messed everything up. I would have killed the emperor right on schedule if not for him. The overseer must understand that."

They reached the barracks and Cordius found himself thrust

through the door. Inside, the long living area was empty save for bunks and footlockers. The guards had no doubt been deployed to search for Cordius, making this the perfect place to hide.

The guard shut the door. "I don't tell the overseer what he must do and neither do you. Get out of that robe. I'll find you a uniform and a razor. When we finish, no one will ever recognize you."

Cordius started to pull his robe off. When the guard turned away, he took out one of his few remaining vials and threw it. It smashed into the back of the man's head, releasing the acid inside and dissolving his skull. He barely made a sound when he collapsed.

Safe now, he finished disrobing. He had only two tricks left. Hopefully they'd be enough to get him out of the palace.

Fifteen minutes later a clean-shaven man in a guard's uniform strode out of the barracks. If he looked a bit old for the job, well, everyone had more important things to worry about. And so Cordius walked right out the front gate without drawing so much as a word of protest.

Now he'd find the overseer and deal with him on his own terms.

CHAPTER 4

Itook longer for Joran and Mia to reach Cordius's lab traveling through the halls than it had traveling via the hidden passages. Having to constantly dodge rushing guards didn't speed the process in the least, but at last they arrived only to find four burly imperial guards standing outside with drawn swords.

To Joran's surprise, they immediately saluted fist to heart and one of them moved to open the door. The guard had barely shifted from his post when a distant explosion shook the palace. Joran had heard that sound often enough to recognize a vial of alchemist's fire exploding. Sounded like Cordius had made his move.

The lab door slammed open and Alexandra emerged. "What was that?"

"Cordius," Joran said. "Sounds like he's in a different wing."

Alexandra frowned. "I felt sure he'd come here. Well, one of the other squads will get him. I've got every unit in the palace on alert. How's Father?"

"Resting comfortably. I had to give him the slow version of

the cure all given how weak he'd become over the course of his illness. You brother is with him."

"Good. Get in here. I want you to look over Cordius's lab and tell me if there's anything I need to do."

Joran and Mia entered the lab and Alexandra slammed the door behind them. It looked exactly how he remembered, which meant Alexandra hadn't touched anything. Thank The One God for that. Mess with the wrong thing in an alchemist's lab and you could get into serious trouble.

"What did Marcus say after I left?" she asked.

"Not much. Once the emperor entered his healing trance, your brother told me to call him by his given name. Shortly after that, we came out and the guard told us to meet you here."

Joran went to the wall and studied it. Where had Cordius touched? He didn't remember exactly.

Mia reached up and tapped the spot. A moment later the niche opened, revealing the steel flask as well as a leather pouch held shut by a string wrapped around a button. Looked like the sort of thing a messenger used.

"Is that the poison?" Alexandra reached for the flask.

"One moment, please." Joran stopped her before she touched the metal.

He got a pouch out of his kit and sprinkled revealing powder on the flask. When nothing happened, he nodded and she grabbed it.

"Light," she said.

"What do we do with it?" Mia asked.

"We'll return it to Fort Death," Alexandra said. "And by we, I mean you two. I want to know exactly what's going on at that fort. If they've been infiltrated, we need to know. This is the second time we've run into the stuff and I'd be delighted if it were the last. But that will have to wait until Father has fully recovered. I want you nearby just in case."

Joran bowed. "I'll need at least that long to go through everything in this room. Will you keep the Black Bile?"

"I'll put it in the family vault. Only Marcus, Father, and I can get into it. There's no safer place in the empire."

"Sounds perfect. If you don't mind, I'd like to keep the guards out front. The fewer people in and out of here, the better."

"I'll arrange three squads of my Iron Guards to rotate through the duty. They'll answer to you, Mia. Anything you need, just ask. The entire palace and staff are at your disposal. I'll expect a nightly report and you'll have to check on Father each morning."

"Understood." Joran cocked his head. "Awfully quiet out there. Someone would have come to let you know if they caught him, right?"

"They'd damn well better. I'm going to see what's happening. You two get to work." Alexandra stalked out, leaving Joran and Mia alone, surrounded by the best-stocked lab in the empire.

"Where do we start?" Mia asked.

"Right there." Joran pointed at the messenger pouch in her hands. "If he hid it in the same place as the poison, it must be important."

"Should I open it?"

"Let me check it for traps first." A quick application of revealing powder and a flick with a small knife severed a hidden thread. "Okay."

Mia unwrapped the string and pulled open the pouch. Inside were three rolled-up scrolls. Another pinch of revealing power showed no further threats. They went to an empty table and unrolled them. Joran took one and Mia another. They read in silence.

"Looks like Cordius was being threatened," Joran said.

"Yeah, by someone called Overseer. Does that name mean anything to you?"

"Not outside of someone managing one of my father's businesses. I seriously doubt that has anything to do with this. We'll ask Alexandra about it tonight. Let's check the third one."

They read together.

"Someone kidnapped his granddaughter. That certainly might make a man betray his emperor," Mia said.

Joran nodded. "It also gives us a place to start looking for him. Someone has to know where the girl lived."

"Do you think she'll make us go looking?" Mia asked.

Joran blew out a sigh. "I hope not. Between inventorying the lab and checking on the emperor, I don't know when I'd find the time. This might be a good chance to get that investigative unit set up. It would take some of the weight off us."

"I don't think Alexandra cares how much weight is on us."

Joran barked a laugh. "No question about that."

No one troubled Joran—including anyone bringing lunch—for the rest of the day as he sorted through shelf after shelf of chemicals. The search for Cordius no doubt kept everyone busy. On the plus side, after spot-checking half a dozen vials, he'd found none tainted or unusable. That said, it would probably be best to just trash everything and rebuild from scratch. The One God knew the empire would have no trouble footing the bill.

He yawned, stretched, and glanced at Mia who had fallen asleep in the room's lone chair. She looked so peaceful he hated to wake her. He also hated to wait any longer for dinner. His stomach won the argument and he shook her by the shoulder.

Her eyes popped open and she reached for her sword before realizing it was Joran who had shaken her. She scrubbed a hand across her face. "Didn't mean to fall asleep."

"That's fine. This is really a one-person job. Under other

circumstances, you'd be better off doing something else, but since we can't be apart..." He shrugged.

She rolled out of the chair and buckled on her sword. "I wouldn't want to be anywhere else. It just got boring."

They left the lab, the Iron Guards saluting as they passed, and made their way back to Alexandra's suite. They met neither guards nor servants, which struck Joran as odd.

"Where is everyone?" Mia asked his question out loud.

Joran shrugged and knocked. A moment later one of the servants opened the door. She chewed her lip and glanced around as if fearful someone might jump out and stab her.

"Is everything alright?" he asked.

"Her Majesty said the assassin hadn't been caught yet. Forgive me, my lord, I didn't mean to leave you standing in the hall."

She stepped aside and Joran led the way in. "Is the princess around?"

"Gone to check on the emperor, I believe. If you're hungry, the kitchen sent sandwiches an hour or so ago."

"Sandwiches sound wonderful. What time is it anyway?"

"The church bell rang seven a few minutes ago." She hurried off to fetch the food.

Joran settled on the couch and Mia joined him. No wonder he was hungry. He hadn't eaten anything in over fourteen hours.

Just as the servant emerged from the back room, the door opened and Alexandra stalked in. She looked angry again. Not unusual, but Joran feared something had happened with the emperor.

"Is he okay?" Joran asked at once.

"Oh, Father's fine. Sleeping like a baby thanks to you. No, I'm angry because the guards lost Cordius. Looks like he shaved and changed his clothes in the barracks before walking out one of the gates. He also murdered six more guards on his way out."

"With the alchemist's fire?"

"Two of them with that, three were stabbed to death, and one had his head half melted by acid." Alexandra sat in an empty chair and snatched up a sandwich as soon as the servant set it on the table.

Joran forgot all about the food. "Cordius stabbed three guards to death? A seventy-year-old man?"

Alexandra froze with the sandwich halfway to her mouth. "Now that you mention it, that is strange. I was so angry and worried that I didn't even think about it. I'll wager the last man he killed murdered those guards then got betrayed for his trouble."

"My thoughts exactly. And the only reason a guard would murder three of his comrades…"

"He's with the traitors," Mia finished. "It wasn't one of the emperor's guards, was it?"

"No, thank The One God." Alexandra turned to Joran. "First thing tomorrow, I want you to interview all three shifts guarding Father's bedchamber. We need to know for sure that they remain loyal to the empire."

Joran nodded as he devoured a ham-and-cheese sandwich. An hour under the influence of a detect-deception potion would handle that, assuming he didn't come across any traitors. If he did, well, best not to think about it.

When she'd finished her first sandwich Alexandra asked, "Did you find anything interesting in Cordius's lab?"

"Yes, though not what I expected to find. It seems the healer had enemies of his own. Blackmailers to be precise. They threatened to kill his granddaughter if he failed to poison the emperor. While I certainly can't condone what he did, I can understand it now. For someone you love, no price is too high."

"I still intend to see him executed, but if we can save the granddaughter, so much the better. Anything else?"

Joran shook his head. "It seems a waste, but I recommend

trashing everything in the lab and getting fresh supplies. The risk any other way is just too high."

"Consider it done. Make a list of everything you need to restore the lab to full function. The servants will handle the purchases. For the time being it's yours. There's no one else I trust to handle the family's health and alchemy needs. Marcus agrees."

Joran's heart leapt. Having a lab like that felt like a dream come true, and even better, Father wouldn't have to pay to stock it. Speaking of which, he really did need to at least send a letter home or better yet pop in for a visit.

"If you can spare me for a couple hours tomorrow, I wanted to check in with my parents."

"Best wait until Father is fully recovered. Once that's done, you'll certainly have earned a day off."

He didn't like it, but arguing would accomplish nothing with Alexandra. And at this point, a few days more or less would make no difference. "What about the corrupt guard?"

"I'll find out all about him in the morning. After you talk to the imperial guards, we'll meet up and the two of you can look into his background. Until I know for sure who I can trust, we'll be handling this matter ourselves."

Joran suppressed a groan and reached for a second sandwich. When she said we, she actually meant him and Mia. His training at the college didn't exactly cover murder investigations, but then again, it hadn't covered killing giant serpents either and that had worked out okay.

Hopefully this would too.

CHAPTER 5

Cordius slumped in the lone chair gracing his hidden lab, utterly exhausted. He'd been wandering Tiber for hours, trying to make sure no one followed him here. When he'd felt confident he didn't have a tail, he made his way to the basement room of a warehouse he owned via a merchant company that didn't know his true identity.

He'd spent a modest portion of his personal fortune building and supplying the place. That task had been simple enough; keeping it secret from the emperor and his many spies took a fair bit more effort. He rubbed his face and frowned at the rough, wrinkled skin. He'd worn a beard for so long he'd forgotten what his face felt like underneath. At least no one would recognize him at a glance.

None of his many problems mattered a fraction as much as what his dear Lovia faced. He needed to find her before word of his failure reached the overseer. Cordius had no idea what the man's real name was or even his true appearance. The two times they'd met, the overseer wore a hooded robe that cast his face in shadow. Only the depth of his voice convinced Cordius he spoke with a man and that might be the result of a potion.

He dared not think about that. It didn't matter in any case. He had wealth enough that he and Lovia could flee to a remote corner of the most distant province and live in comfort for the rest of her life. Surely the overseer had better things to do than hunt down an old man and his granddaughter.

His humorless chuckle sounded bitter in the silent room. No, if he betrayed the overseer, death would certainly hunt him for the rest of his days. Unless, of course, the hunter ended up dead first.

Forcing himself out of his chair, Cordius marched over to the workbench with grim determination. He might have trained primarily as a healer, but he knew enough about alchemy to brew up weapons to reduce the overseer and his henchmen to smoking ruins.

First, he reached for the precursor to alchemist's fire then he caught himself. Satisfying as he'd find torching everything between himself and his granddaughter, Lovia might get caught in the backdraft. Not to mention the danger of drawing all the emperor's soldiers down on his head. Something subtler would be necessary.

By the time ten bells had rung, Cordius had a neat row of vials filled with many flavors of death lined up on his workbench. His eyes drooped and much as he'd like to go at once to find his contact, force the pig to tell him where his allies held Lovia, and kill everyone between him and her, he didn't dare in his exhausted state.

A few hours' sleep then at first light he'd set out. And woe to anyone that stood in his way.

———

Eight bells woke Cordius from a dead sleep. So much for getting an early start. In the plays, the hero always set out at dawn. He rolled out of his cot, winced as he stood, and smiled at his own stupidity. He was no hero, just a broken-down old man that had betrayed everything he believed in for the only family he had left. And if put in that situation again, he'd make the exact same decision. As long as Lovia stayed safe, nothing else mattered, including the emperor's life.

He took a step toward the workbench and grimaced. Between the chase and his sleeping arrangements, his entire body felt like he'd been beaten with a knotted stick. He tried to avoid using potions for his aches and pains; the most effective ones also carried a risk of addiction. But today that didn't matter. He needed to be at his best.

Three painful steps brought him to a cabinet filled with healing potions. He took an acid-green one, pulled the lid, and sniffed. Spearmint, good, this was the one he wanted. He threw it back and ten seconds later felt like a young man again. Strength and vitality flowed through him and would for twelve hours. Then he'd crash hard, reduced to little more than a still-breathing corpse for a day.

Unless he took another dose.

Having no idea how long he'd need to find his granddaughter and escape Tiber, Cordius pocketed two more of the potions. If he had to use both of them, he'd end up a corpse and not the still-breathing kind.

Next, he found his combat harness and filled its many loops with vials. When he had his arsenal in place, he hid it with a loose-fitting robe whose hood would also help disguise his features. Finally, a small pouch of silver coins to buy his breakfast went into a pocket and he set out.

The lab stairs exited into an unused closet near the rear of the warehouse. He slipped out, ignoring the many workers already busy shouting and loading wagons. The manager knew that the building's crazy owner valued his privacy and made sure his employees stayed well away from the entrance.

Outside, he strode down the narrow street, keeping close to the buildings to let passing wagons go by. Three blocks brought him close enough to the food stands to smell frying dough and roasting meat. His mouth watered and he pulled two coins out for a small beer and a meat pie. His favorite vendor handed the food over without a word as she accepted the coins. The woman never spoke so far as he'd noticed; that's what made her his favorite.

Eating as he walked, Cordius considered his best approach. He'd never actually sought out his contact before, usually the man came to him. Always in the same neighborhood, so Cordius would start there. The One God owed him some luck after everything that had happened.

He finished his breakfast and brushed the crumbs off his face. The priests would say that The One God owed no one anything. We all owed him for our very existence. Be that as it may, Cordius still hoped he took mercy on a desperate old man. For Lovia's sake if not his own.

When he reached the target neighborhood, a middle-class area filled with three- and four-story apartment buildings where doubtless many of the teamsters at the warehouse lived, he reached into his robe and pulled out a vial filled with paralyzing powder. He wanted to question the man, not kill him.

At least not right away.

One of the reasons he'd planned to get here early was to blend in with the people headed out to work. Now he found the streets largely empty save for a few women dressed in tan tunics, walking and chatting while their children ran around screaming.

He found the scene both soothing and annoying. Why should these people get to have a normal life when his had fallen apart? A little, bitter piece of him wanted to hurl a vial of Dread Spores at them just to watch the group die screaming. He dismissed that idea at once. They'd done nothing deserving of his wrath. Better to quickly find someone that had.

He put a few blocks between himself and the mothers and children. His contact had to be around here somewhere.

No sooner had the thought entered his head when something sharp poked him in the back. "Just keep walking," a familiar voice said.

How had his contact snuck up on him without Cordius noticing something? Perhaps an invisibility potion. He didn't know and it didn't matter.

A sharp poke in the ribs turned him toward a brick bakery that appeared closed up and abandoned. "In there."

Cordius obliged, turning toward the door. As he moved, he broke the seal on his vial and worked his nail into the cork.

"Open the door," his contact said.

Cordius reached out with his free hand and pulled. As he did, he turned, popped the cork out, and flung a paralyzing potion into his contact's face.

The man slashed once, opening a bloody gash in Cordius's side before his body started to stiffen.

Grabbing his would-be kidnapper by the collar, Cordius forced him into the bakery before he went fully rigid. The effects of his earlier potion kept the pain from his wound to a minimum, but he'd need to apply troll's blood paste soon.

His contact collapsed to the floor. Cordius ignored him and saw to his injury. The paste sealed it quickly, leaving only a thin line and a bloodstain behind. He had enough paste for three more cuts like that. He winced and hoped he wouldn't need it even as he feared he'd need that much and more before he finished his business.

A swift kick turned the paralyzed man over on his back. He glared up at Cordius. This variation of the poison left the target's head free to move and speak.

"I know you think you won't tell me anything." Cordius

drank a detect-deception potion. "But you will. The only question is how much pain will it cost you?"

The man's jaw muscles bunched as he clenched his teeth together. A stubborn one. Pity. Cordius didn't generally like inflicting pain, but this once he'd rethink his preferences.

A vial of acid nearly the same color as the vitality potion he took earlier slid out of his harness. Cordius carefully pulled out the cork.

"Where is my granddaughter?"

No reply.

Shaking his head, he let a drop fall on the man's cheek. Skin sizzled as the acid did its work. His contact hissed then groaned as the acid burned through his cheek, leaving a hole big enough for Cordius's finger.

"Where is she?"

Still nothing. He had to give the man credit for toughness if not brains. The next drop landed on his lip and burned through before dissolving two of his front teeth.

"If you don't tell me where Lovia is, the next one is going in your left eye. I've attended a few inquisitions. Believe me, you don't want me to dissolve your eyes. The prisoners always scream like mad when that happens. But the best part is, when I'm done, I can give you a potion of regeneration. Growing your eyes back is every bit as painful as melting them, or so I'm told."

His contact trembled so hard his teeth chattered. "I don't know where she is, I swear. Only the overseer knows."

A bit of truth at last. "That's a start. Where can I find the overseer?"

"A little villa in the second ring. It's called The Snow Bird since it's painted white. It's the only white house on Fourth Street, you can't miss it."

More truth, good, nothing like a couple drops of acid to motivate a man. "Thank you very much."

Cordius dumped the vial of acid on his contact's face and

head. The screams didn't end until most of his brain resembled a melted candle. Thank goodness for thick brick walls. He had no desire to attract attention. No doubt his now-dead contact chose this place for similar reasons.

Cordius very much looked forward to giving the overseer a taste of what he'd fed his minion.

CHAPTER 6

Joran and Mia walked down the sidewalk through one of the nicer neighborhoods in Tiber's second ring. The guard they assumed had betrayed his fellows—Kellic, according to the palace scribe Joran spoke to—only to be killed by Cordius, lived in the area. The houses all had two stories, fresh coats of paint, and a few even had yards.

Joran's apartment was actually in this ring, though on the opposite side of the city. Mother had been horrified that he'd chosen to live in the second ring. "Slumming," she called it. No noble worth the name would live there, she said. Which explained why he'd moved there.

And now he found himself living in the palace while attending the emperor himself, his formal post being personal advisor to the princess. Nobility surrounded him on all sides though happily most were kept at a distance for now. The effort he'd expended avoiding them for the past four years seemed like a complete waste of time. But they had been good times.

"What do you think we'll find?" Mia asked.

Joran banished his gloomy thoughts and forced a smile. "Beats me. I'm impressed Kellic could afford a place in this part of the city. Guard sergeants must make good coin at the palace. Though apparently not enough to purchase more than passing loyalty. There it is."

They stopped in front of a white house surrounded by a wrought iron fence. A little sign marked it as number sixty. That matched what the scribe said. Joran shook his head. He knew lesser nobles that lived in worse-looking places than this. Anyone making more than a cursory effort would realize something strange was going on.

Mia reached around, popped the latch, and they strode through. Joran plucked his official amulet out of his tunic and let it rest on his chest where it flashed in the sunlight. Only an idiot or a traitor would give someone wearing a platinum amulet marked with the imperial eagle any trouble.

Joran knocked on the freshly painted red door. Seconds later a very pregnant woman dressed in a neatly pressed white silk robe opened the door. "Who are you and why are you loitering on my doorstep?"

He pointed at the amulet and her eyes seemed to rapidly double in size. "Please forgive me, my lord. My husband didn't come home last night and I'm a bit of a mess. Are...Are you here about Kellic?"

"In a manner of speaking," Joran said. "Can we come inside? This may take a moment and I'm sure you'd prefer to sit."

"Thank you for your consideration. Please come in."

She led them through a small foyer to a nearby sitting room. Joran and Mia sat on a patterned loveseat while she practically collapsed in a chair. A silver bell sat on a fine hardwood coffee table between them. She rang it and a moment later a rather plain, blond provincial woman wearing a leather slave collar and white tunic hurried in.

"Yes, Mistress?" the slave girl asked.

"Tea and snacks for our guests. Quickly now." The slave hurried back out and sounds came from what Joran assumed to be the kitchen. She turned her attention back to Joran and Mia. "What can I do for you?"

How did one best tell a woman about to give birth that her husband not only got himself murdered, but also served a cult dedicated to the empire's destruction? Directly seemed best. Hopefully she didn't miscarry.

"There's no easy way to say this. Kellic was killed yesterday." She gasped and her hand went immediately to her swollen abdomen. Taking a breath, Joran continued. "It seems he'd fallen in with a dangerous group that call themselves followers of The One True God. Does that mean anything to you?"

"No, I've never heard the phrase before. Kellic always went to work early and came home early. As far as I know he went nowhere else and had few friends outside of the other guards. We went to church every God's Day. He couldn't..." She broke down and started crying.

Joran grimaced. Weeping females weren't his area of expertise.

The slave girl chose that moment to return with a silver tray laden with cups, crackers covered with cheese, and a steaming tea pot. "Mistress, is all well?"

The woman wiped her eyes and sat up straight. "Yes, I'm fine now. These people just brought some unfortunate news. Go ahead and serve."

The tray clinked down on the table and she poured the tea, handing each of them a cup. Joran took his to be polite, but he had no intention of drinking. One of his mother's constant warnings was to never trust anything prepared by a slave if they didn't have a free person overseeing their work. You were asking for trouble if you did. While Joran didn't always hold to everything his mother taught, that had always seemed a prudent bit of advice.

The slave finished and withdrew, leaving them alone once

more. At least Kellic's wife appeared to have herself back under control, thank The One God.

Mia glanced his way, then at the cup, then back at him. Joran gave a slight shake of his head. Better safe than sorry.

After the wife had taken a big gulp, they all set their cups back down. "I don't know what I can tell you. Kellic never spoke about his work. He didn't think it appropriate to discuss it with a woman, even his wife. Perhaps now I know why. What will happen to us?"

"I don't know. I'll recommend some sort of pension, at least until the child is grown, but given the circumstances of your husband's death, the palace may have other ideas. Is coin an issue? This is a very nice home in an equally nice neighborhood."

"It's been in my family for generations, a leftover from when we were more prosperous. Kellic made enough to take care of it and pay the taxes. I suppose I'll have to sell it. Jenna too. Shame really, but the coin should keep us comfortable for many years."

Joran was getting the distinct impression that they were wasting their time. "Well. I'm sorry to have been the bearer of bad news. We'll leave you alone."

He stood and Mia quickly joined him. Out of the corner of his eye he caught a glimpse of the slave peeking at them from the shadows of the kitchen doorway. She ducked out of sight at once. The servants always wanted to know what transpired in their household. Joran didn't blame her considering her fate rested on the family's success or lack thereof as the case may be.

The fate of a slave was yet another thing outside of his control. The wife didn't bother getting up, so they showed themselves out.

As soon as they reached the street Mia said, "I don't envy her."

"Neither do I." Joran set out with no particular destination in mind.

Alexandra didn't expect a report until dinner time and he had no desire to rush back to the palace. Not to mention they hadn't actually learned anything, except Kellic had married the least lucky woman in the city.

"Where are we going?" Mia asked.

"Nowhere. I thought a little walk might clear my head. We're no closer to finding Overseer than we were this morning. Maybe inspiration will strike." He looked her way. Mia's eyes were narrow and her hand inched toward her sword hilt. "What?"

"Someone's following us."

"The slave girl?" Joran asked.

"Maybe. Why do you guess her?"

"She was watching us from the kitchen when we left. Beyond that it was only a guess. Should we see what she wants?"

"I would very much like to know."

An explosion from further north cut the discussion short. Joran knew that sound all too well. Someone had set off a vial of alchemist's fire and he had a pretty good idea who.

They shared a look and ran toward the smoke, the slave girl forgotten.

———

Cordius stood behind a tree across from The Snow Bird and wished he had the chemicals necessary to brew an invisibility potion. But you couldn't have everything. He'd manage somehow. Assuming the overseer had Lovia in there—a thin possibility, he acknowledged—then he'd get her out or die trying.

Walking up to the unguarded front door seemed a poor idea. He glanced up and down the street. No one in sight. A lucky break that. The locals had probably gone off to work for the day. Even the lower-ranking nobles that called the neighborhood home had to do something to support their semi-lavish lifestyles.

Not that Cordius knew much about that. He'd spent most of his time tending the royal family. The lower-ranking nobles interested him not in the least. As he stood in an unfamiliar part of the city trying to figure out how to raid an equally unfamiliar house, he found he wished he'd expanded his studies beyond healing and alchemy.

He shrugged and pulled out a vial of alchemist's fire. When in doubt, cause a distraction.

Cordius hurried up to the front door, knocked, and ran back to his hiding place. As he did so he gave a word of thanks for the vitality potion he'd drunk before leaving his hidden lab. That extra strength would serve him well.

The door opened and a liveried servant in his midfifties peered left and right.

Cordius threw the vial with all his might right at the man.

The explosion sent the door flying one way and the servant's body another. The front of the house started burning and a pillar of black smoke rose into the sky.

Guards and the fire brigade would arrive soon. Hopefully he and Lovia could use the chaos to escape, assuming he found her.

He sprinted across the street and through the burning entrance. His cloak had a special treatment that made it fire resistant. That would be useful today. In his right hand he clutched a vial of paralyzing powder. Ready as possible, he glanced around the entrance. Smoke already filled it, but he spotted the stairs easily enough. Would she be on the second floor? No, probably the basement would be better.

"Hey!" someone shouted from the top of the stairs.

Four guards stomped toward him, their boots raising a terrible racket.

Cordius threw the vial. It shattered on the lead guard's face and powder went everywhere. The guards' bodies stiffened and they tumbled down the rest of the stairs. He knelt beside the nearest man, a second vial of acid in his hands. His interrogation technique had worked well the first time. Hopefully it would a second time.

"Where is the master of the house?" Cordius asked. "Answer quickly and honestly or so help me I'll melt your face right down to the skull."

"Downstairs, sir. He has a workshop. There's also a tunnel that connects the house to a storehouse up the street. Please, I only work here. I have a family, two kids."

All the truth. Since he had no interest in killing ignorant guards, he left the men where they lay and hurried back toward the kitchen. Most buildings with basements had an access point in the kitchen. He swapped his acid for more paralyzing powder. It acted faster and had a wider area of effect. Should he run into another group of guards he'd be far better off with that.

Sure enough, he found the kitchen empty and stairwell door open. No doubt the servants had fled when the explosion went off. He started down, careful of his footing. A dim, golden light from below provided just enough illumination to keep him from breaking his neck.

Shouts from above indicated that the guards had arrived. Good, they'd keep the fire from spreading. Cordius had no desire to burn down the entire neighborhood.

At the bottom of the steps a stone passage led to an open door in the far wall. It looked like the entrance to a tunnel. That had to be what the guard described. Hopefully the overseer wasn't that far ahead.

He pulled out a blue light vial and shook it until it glowed bright enough to reveal the roughhewn tunnel. It went down then flattened out. Fresh tracks indicated people had been here not long ago. He hurried on, eager for the final confrontation.

The tunnel ran for far longer than Cordius had expected. He finally emerged in a warehouse filled with crates and baskets filled with some sort of produce. He ignored them and focused on two people, a man and a woman, seated in what looked like a reception area to his right. He knew Lovia at once and praised The One God she appeared unharmed. The man seated beside her held a shining dagger nearly long enough to be called a shortsword. He wore a well-trimmed beard, blue tunic, and black trousers. Whether the overseer himself or one of his lackeys Cordius neither knew nor cared.

He put his blue light vial away, pulled a vial of alchemist's fire to go with his paralyzing powder, and strode over to the pair. Halfway there a rumble shook the building. Cordius turned to see six more guards dressed in leather armor standing beside the tunnel entrance from which dust billowed.

Cordius swallowed the lump in his throat. No going back that way.

He continued toward Lovia. Her captor still hadn't spoken or made a move. Whatever his game, Cordius had no interest in playing.

The guards started toward him. Cordius raised the vial of alchemist's fire. "Unless you wish to burn to death, I suggest you keep your distance."

They froze. Cordius shifted his approach, keeping both the guards and Lovia and her captor in sight. A few paces away he stopped. "I just want my granddaughter. Let us go and there will be no more trouble."

"This should have been an easy task." The man spoke at last. "As the emperor's personal healer, who would dare suggest you'd betray him? Yet still you failed. Very disappointing. I thought you'd do anything for Lovia."

"I would, including killing you in the most painful way I can think of." Cordius ground his teeth. "It wasn't my fault. The princess's advisor examined him and smelled the Black Bile. She believed him and somehow convinced the prince. What was I supposed to do?"

"Joran Den Cade. It seems he might be a problem." The man scratched his chin, ignoring Cordius completely.

"Hey! No more talking. Get away from her and let us walk away. Anything else and I swear—"

"Oh, Grandfather," Lovia said. "Don't you understand? No one kidnapped me. This was all my plan. If only you'd succeeded, my place in the cult would have been assured. You'd have earned me a place of power and status in the new world. Now I have to find another way to prove my worth."

Cordius stared, not fully believing what he heard. "You used me? Why? I'd have given you anything."

"I know, but you never would have betrayed the emperor for me, not willingly. Your place in the palace was all I had to negotiate with. The overseer liked my plan, but now I have no idea what he might do with me."

The man with the dagger reached out and squeezed her hand. "Don't worry. The plan's failure can't be blamed on you. The overseer isn't the sort to kill a potentially useful follower for something out of her control." Turning to Cordius, the man said, "Now, how about you set those vials down? Your place at the palace is lost, but your knowledge and skill would still be a great asset for us. Bringing down the empire will take the efforts of many skilled people. Will you join us?"

"Will you join me?" Lovia asked.

Cordius's head spun. He'd betrayed the man that raised him up to the highest position a healer in the empire could aspire to and all for a lie. His Lovia, the light of his life, was a traitor to the empire and he'd seen nothing. Either his mind had gone or he didn't want to see. He wished for the former but knew it was the latter.

"No, I don't think I will." He hurled the vial of alchemist's fire at his feet. Better if he died here trying to fix his mistake. He might find some honor in that.

Six inches from the floor the vial stopped.

Cordius stared as it flew over to the unnamed man, settling harmlessly in his empty hand. "Surprised? You're not the only one that knows a trick or two. Guards! Take him."

"Gently," Lovia added. "Grandfather may yet be persuaded to do the right thing."

As the guards moved to surround him, Cordius flung the paralyzing powder in every direction. He'd long since made himself immune to the stuff.

As the guards collapsed, he ran for the door in the front of the warehouse.

He staggered, a sharp pain in his side nearly sending him to his knees. Lucky for him the effects of his earlier potion allowed him to push through and stumble out into the street. A few people stared then hurried away.

Cordius didn't blame them. In fact, hurrying away seemed like a fine idea. Something warm ran down his side. When he looked, he saw the end of a hand crossbow bolt sticking out of him. His alchemically treated robes had slowed it enough that only an inch pierced his flesh, but that still hurt, nearly as badly as Lovia's betrayal.

He shuffled away. There had to be more guards around and Cordius wanted to be anywhere else when they came looking for him.

CHAPTER 7

Joran and Mia stopped a short distance from the source of the smoke, a fully engulfed building surrounded by a mix of guards and a bucket brigade ten men long. The heat and roar of the flames convinced Joran to keep his distance. The firefighters had little hope of saving the house, but it looked like they would succeed in keeping the fire from spreading. In a city the size of Tiber, you could hope for little better.

He tapped the nearest guard on a soot-stained shoulder.

The man rounded on him, looking ready to bawl him out. One look at Joran, or most likely his amulet, and the guard's expression softened. "Can I help you, my lord?"

"What happened here?"

"Too soon to say. My squad heard the explosion and came running. The house was already burning when we arrived. We did manage to drag a few survivors out before it got out of control. One poor bastard—beg pardon, ma'am—looked like he'd been right in the center of the blast. Nothing left but a charred body."

Joran frowned. Not Cordius. He had too much experience to

get caught in his own blast. Did the renegade target this place for some reason? Seemed likely, but Joran had no idea why.

"Do you know who owns this place?" Joran asked.

"No idea, my lord. Some of the locals might."

Mia tugged on his sleeve.

Since he had no more questions Joran said, "Thank you, Guardsman."

When the man had turned his attention back to the fire Joran said, "What is it?"

"There's someone over there. I saw a flash of white before they ducked into an alley."

"The slave girl again?"

"Don't think so. From the build I'd say it was a man kind of hunched over. I smelled blood on him from here."

Joran nodded. "Worth a look. Best be ready just in case whoever spilled his blood decides to try and spill ours."

Mia drew her sword and Joran pulled a paralyzing potion from one of his hidden pockets. She led the way up the street and down an alley between two shops. The owner of one of them, an old man with a massive gut and long white beard, stood on his porch watching the fire.

"Excuse me, sir. Did you see someone pass by a moment ago?" Joran asked.

"I did. He looked drunk. I swear this neighborhood is going straight to hell. Ten years ago we didn't have fires or drunks wandering the street. If you catch him, drag him off to the guard-house to sleep it off. Business is bad enough as it is." So saying, the merchant strode back into his shop and slammed the door.

"I fear his personality may have something to do with the lack of business," Mia said.

"Maybe, but I'll wager he treats his customers a good deal better than two strangers. Come on."

Mia led the way down the alley, sword raised and ready. A

figure in white lay propped up against the shop's wall. His head hung, obscuring his face, but from the visible white hair and wrinkles, Joran suspected they'd found their man.

"Cordius?" Joran asked.

The old man looked up at them and offered a pained smile. "It would be you that found me. Your meddling has caused me no end of trouble."

"I suspect you poisoning the emperor contributed to your woes. I know you were being blackmailed; I found the scrolls you hid. Tell us everything and maybe I can convince the princess to be merciful."

Mia shot him a disbelieving look. He didn't blame her. In truth, Joran doubted anything would keep Alexandra and her brother from extracting a very painful retribution for what Cordius did to their father.

"You lie poorly," Cordius said. "But I'll tell you anyway. Not that I know—"

A dagger slammed into Cordius's chest, silencing him forever.

Joran didn't have time to get a word out before Mia sprinted for the mouth of the alley.

The clash of steel on steel filled the air.

Nothing Joran did would help Cordius now. He left the rapidly cooling body and hurried to the end of the alley. Mia and the slave girl, Jenna, fought in the street. It seemed impossible, but somehow Jenna met every blow and turned it aside. She wielded a pair of curved shortswords with consummate skill. She had also traded her slave tunic for a gray, one-piece bodysuit. He'd never seen anything like it.

Mia appeared to be holding back, probably in the hope that she might get a new prisoner to replace the dead one.

He fingered the vial of paralyzing powder and debated stepping in.

No, better if he kept his eyes open. Jenna might have friends. Besides, Mia didn't look like she was in immediate danger.

Three more rapid clashes and Mia brought her sword down on Jenna's left arm. The bone snapped, but the edge didn't bite. Whatever the suit was made of, it resisted imperial steel.

Mia bore in on her now one-armed opponent. A hard left-to-right swing sent the curved sword in Jenna's right hand flying.

A quick blow to the temple put Jenna down.

"Fat lot of help you were," Mia said as he approached.

"I debated intervening, but figured watching for reinforcements was more important seeing as you weren't having too hard a time."

"I should have beaten her in seconds. How did she keep up with me and for that matter how is her left arm still attached?"

"Excellent questions. Unfortunately, I have no idea how she did either of those things. I am looking forward to figuring it out, assuming we can find some guards to drag her back to the palace dungeon. Honestly, I'm feeling worse and worse for Kellic's wife."

Mia sheathed her sword. "At least we know how Kellic communicated with his superiors."

"Do we? I assume Jenna served as a threat over his head. Behave or your wife's dead. I doubt she often left the house. Kellic must have gotten his orders some other way. At a minimum we need to assume there are other traitors in the palace."

"If you're right, how will we know who to trust?"

"For the moment, I trust you and the imperial family. Until I've interviewed them personally with a detect-deception potion active, everyone else is suspect."

Joran ended up pressing a squad of guards into service to transport Jenna and Cordius's body back to the palace. Not the most pleasant walk through the city he'd ever made, but at last the former healer was in the morgue and the would-be assassin stripped naked and locked in a cell. He didn't dare try and guess if they were ahead or behind, but at least they had someone to question, assuming she woke up from the blow Mia struck.

Mia led the way out of the rather dank, moldy dungeon and up into the palace proper. Joran took a deep breath of fresh air and they turned toward Alexandra's suite. He wanted to interview the servants just to be sure. Even though they usually kept them a safe distance when discussing anything important, Joran's paranoia demanded he make sure. Especially since dinner would be served soon and he wanted to eat. The thought of having one of the girls poison his food did nothing for his appetite.

At least things here seemed to have gotten back to something resembling normal. Servants bustled through the halls, a guard patrol passed, saluting when they saw Joran. Word of his position seemed to have spread. Whether that turned out to be useful or just painted a target on his back remained to be seen. Mia studied each person they passed with narrow, focused eyes. The sort of eyes that filled him with confidence that she'd deal with anyone looking to cause trouble.

They reached the door to Alexandra's suite without any catastrophes befalling them. That suited Joran fine as he'd had plenty for today. Since they basically lived here now, Mia didn't bother knocking before pushing the door open. They found the sitting room empty and no sign of the servants.

Barely had he thought it when one of the rear doors opened and three of the serving girls came trotting out. May as well get started.

Joran fished the correct vial out of his kit, drank it, and asked the first girl, "Are you now or have you ever, in thought or deed, betrayed the empire?"

She stared at him with wide dark eyes, her hands trembling as she twisted the hem of her tunic. "Never, my lord. Her Majesty has given me a far better life than I ever dared hope for."

No lie. Good. "Has anyone ever contacted you seeking information about the palace or mentioned anything negative about the church?"

"No, never."

Joran nodded and smiled to show that she wasn't in trouble. He would have liked to ask specifically about The One True God cult, but didn't want to risk the name getting out amongst the servants before he had a chance to interview the rest of them.

He repeated the questions with the rest of the servants, including the ones that didn't immediately emerge from the bedroom they shared. They all passed with flying colors. Thank The One God for that. Now he had a few people he trusted to look after things.

"I apologize if my questions upset you, ladies," Joran said. "But I had to be certain of your loyalty. I'm sure you heard about the excitement yesterday."

They were all staring at him, looking nervous, clearly not sure what he planned to ask them to do. Doubtless no one had ever questioned them, much less spoken to them in such a serious tone. In Joran's experience nobles tended to look at servants about the same way they did furniture.

"We heard some guards died and the chief healer had gone missing." The first girl he questioned seemed to have taken on the role of spokeswoman. She looked like the youngest of the group, but she had gumption. He liked that.

"That's right. We had a traitor in our midst and our lack of care ended up getting good people killed. No one wants that to happen again. Therefore, we'll be questioning everyone in the palace, just to be sure no more enemies are hiding among us. Now that I've confirmed your loyalty, Her Majesty, Mia, and I are going to be counting on you."

The girls drew themselves up, puffing out their chests in an attractive display of pride.

"What can we do, my lord?" the spokeswoman asked.

"What's your name?" Joran asked.

Her jaw dropped. Joran was probably the first nobleman that had ever asked her name. "Marsa, my lord."

"Well, Marsa, until I finish with the kitchen staff, you'll be in charge of preparing all our meals. I also need you to keep your ears open while you're out in the palace. If you hear anything strange, no matter how small, tell me. We have to work together, all of us, to keep our empire safe. No task is too small. Do you understand?" He looked at all of them as he asked that final question.

They all nodded, seeming well pleased with his speech. And he meant every word. Servants heard everything and the more they had listening, the better.

"Good. Now, when Her Majesty returns, she will likely be hungry. Marsa, would you take two of the others and see about dinner? If anyone gives you trouble, tell them that Princess Alexandra asked you to handle the cooking herself."

Marsa grabbed two of the girls and rushed out, clearly eager to begin her mission. The remaining servants looked at him expectantly. Joran hated to disappoint, but he had nothing for them to do at the moment.

Fortunately, the door opened and Alexandra strode in, sparing him the need to think of something. As soon as they saw her the girls scurried away to their room.

"Why are three of my servants leaving the suite?" Alexandra asked.

Joran explained, adding, "I'll check some alchemists this evening and get them to help with the vetting, but until I'm sure of the kitchen staff, I figured better not to risk our food."

"If the family's most trusted servant and healer hadn't just tried to kill my father, I might worry that you were overly cautious. As it stands, I'm glad you thought of it as an assassin in the kitchen never crossed my mind. Now, I assume you have a report to make?"

Joran told her everything that had happened since they left that morning. "I don't know how Kellic's wife will manage now. Cordius can't tell us anything, though before the assassin killed him, he admitted he knew little. I'm hopeful she'll be of more use."

"How hopeful?" Alexandra asked.

"Not as hopeful as I'd like. Some of these cultists seem very dedicated to their cause. Certainly they show no hesitation to use anyone possible. I can't help wondering what their leader has promised them. Samaritan clearly acted out of hatred of the empire. Cordius was blackmailed. Kellic's wife appeared to be under threat from Jenna which explains his decisions. But Jenna herself is the real mystery. Is there some way to tell if she's a real slave and if so who sold her?"

"Probably, but I never had much to do with slaves. We keep none in the palace; too big a risk." Alexandra laughed at that. "Much good our precautions did. Tomorrow I want you to focus on getting a team set up to vet the palace guards and servants. If this assassin wakes up, we'll interrogate her. Otherwise, Father should wake the day after tomorrow and no doubt he'll have many questions."

Joran smiled. "It would be nice if we had some answers for him."

CHAPTER 8

When morning rolled around and Jenna still hadn't woken, Joran ended up taking a break from interviewing alchemists to fix her a very mild healing potion. Now he stood beside Mia and Alexandra in the dank dungeon waiting for it to kick in. They'd ended up moving the prisoner from the original cell to one in the isolation wing of the dungeon. Joran hadn't even known the dungeon came with different wings, but yes, there were several, depending on your prisoner and what you wanted to do to them. The isolation wing had divided cells with really thick walls so no one could hear anything from outside.

"Your brother didn't want to join us, Majesty?" Mia asked.

"Marcus hasn't left Father's side since the fight with Cordius. He even sleeps in there. Not that I think he sleeps much."

"Very devoted," Joran said.

Alexandra snorted. "Marcus really doesn't want to be emperor. He's been praying so hard for Father to recover, I suspect The One God is sick of hearing from him. What about you? Find any more traitors?"

"Not yet. I've spoken to all the alchemists that serve in the palace and they're all loyal. I've got them spread out checking the servants and guards. My best guess is that we won't find any more people loyal to the cult. Once word got out that we'd begun the search, most likely they vanished into the city, never to be seen again. That's how we'll know just how many traitors we had."

"Let's hope it's zero," Mia said.

Joran shook his head. Zero would be nice, but he suspected the actual number would be higher.

Jenna groaned and sat up as the potion took effect. He'd done his best to make it just strong enough for her to speak, but not strong enough to repair her broken arm. Judging from the way she clutched it to her side, he'd succeeded.

"Why is she naked again?" Alexandra asked.

"Because naked people have a harder time hiding poison, firebombs, explosives, and other unpleasant surprises." Joran shrugged. "As I said, I've become paranoid."

"Where?" Jenna asked. "How?"

"You're in the palace dungeon," Alexandra said. "Since you deprived me of the chance to kill Cordius, I'm considering taking my frustration out on you. That is, unless you tell me something that will change my mind."

Jenna stood and scrubbed her face. If being naked in front of three strangers made her uncomfortable she hid it well. "I have nothing to say."

Joran wished there was a potion to make people talk as well as one that let you hear lies. Maybe that would be his next research project, assuming he ever got to research anything again.

"Do you have so much faith in them?" Mia asked. "How can you imagine your little cult is strong enough to defeat the entire empire?"

"It's kind of a sad delusion," Joran agreed.

"There will always be those that hate the empire," Alexandra said. "And there will always be those that hunt them down. For over five hundred years one group or another has tried to defeat us and we're still here."

"And that is why we will succeed." Jenna stared at them with hate-filled eyes. "Your arrogance makes you blind to reality. We've found secrets, magic you can't begin to imagine. The One True God has shown us the way. We will see your empire reduced to ashes and something better put in its place. Something the people of the world can be proud of."

It was a longer speech than Joran expected, but hardly revealing. "Is the gray outfit you wore some of this special magic?"

Jenna said nothing. Her bare bottom made a meaty smack when she sat on the cold stone floor.

"I wonder," Joran muttered as he shrugged out of his kit.

He shook some revealing powder into his hand and puffed it out so the dust settled over Jenna. Little sparks shot out wherever it hit her skin.

"Some sort of magic has been used on her, though I can't tell what. Looks like a permanent effect." He glanced at Mia. "Try and cut her, just a shallow slash, nothing lethal."

"What are you thinking?" Alexandra asked.

"I wonder if the outfit she wore or her own power stopped Mia's sword from cutting. I'm still confident it was the outfit since her arm broke, but I wish to be sure. You don't mind, do you?"

"Not at all. We're going to start cutting on her at some point. Might as well see if we actually can."

Jenna scrambled to her feet and took up a crouch as Mia moved closer to the bars.

"Hold your arm out and I promise to only scratch you," Mia said.

Jenna backed up as far as the cell allowed. "If you want to cut me, you're going to earn it."

Mia made a lightning-fast thrust through the bars and Jenna dodged. When she did, some of the remaining powder sparked.

When Jenna tried to grab Mia's wrist, she jerked back out of the cell.

"She's quick," Alexandra said.

"Yes. I'm confident that whatever magic her superiors used enhanced her speed and strength enough to keep up with Mia. The garment must be what protected her from the sword. We can test that later. Thank you, Mia, that was perfect."

She grinned and sheathed her sword. "That was amazing. I knew just what you wanted without you even saying anything."

Joran nodded. Their soul bond grew stronger all the time. "Majesty, I advise you to execute her right in that cell. Without knowing the full breadth of her abilities, taking her out is too risky."

"Agreed, though I hate letting her get off so easily."

"You think it will be that easy!" Jenna screamed like a mad thing.

Joran pulled a black vial of dread spores out of his kit. "With your permission, Majesty?"

Alexandra nodded and Joran threw the vial so it smashed in front of the cell.

They quickly fled the isolation chamber as the black cloud spread, filling the space. In less than a minute the spores did their work and went inert, falling to the floor. Jenna lay on the cold stone, unmoving.

"Check her," Alexandra said.

Mia went in and ran Jenna through the back, piercing her heart. If she wasn't dead before, she certainly was now.

"I've had enough for today. I want to be well rested when Father wakes in the morning."

Joran seconded that idea, though he feared his dreams would not be pleasant ones tonight.

CHAPTER 9

Alexandra chewed her lip, paced, and looked from her sleeping father to her fretting brother. Marcus sat beside the bed still dressed in the same outfit he'd worn the day they learned Cordius had turned traitor. He didn't exactly stink, but he clearly hadn't bathed or washed his hair in days. Alexandra had offered to sit with Father while he got cleaned up, but Marcus refused. He seemed to trust no one else to watch over Father. She found that odd given his total lack of sword skill.

No, that was unkind. His fear just took a different shape from hers. Alexandra wanted to hunt down all those responsible, while Marcus preferred to focus on protecting what he cared about. Same destination, just different paths.

She'd ordered Joran and Mia to wait out in the hall. If Father wanted to speak to them, she'd bring them in then. For now she wanted no one seeing him so weak. Not that they both hadn't already seen him, but he'd been unconscious for that and so felt no embarrassment.

The color had come back to his cheeks and his breathing sounded strong and deep, both good signs. Not that she harbored any doubts about Joran's ability as a healer. He'd already proven himself to her plenty of times. Were it her life on the line, she'd want no one else tending her.

"Why doesn't he wake?" Marcus asked. "It's been more than three days."

"Joran says the cure all doesn't work on an exact timetable. It varies depending on the severity of the illness or injury. Since Father had been dosed repeatedly with the most lethal poison on the planet, he might need an extra hour or two. You must admit he looks much better."

"He does. I just want him to open his eyes and speak to me. I want to hear his voice and know he's cured. Until that happens, I can't relax. I can't think of anything else."

"Well, you'd better think of something else. Between your absence from court and our hunt for traitors, the nobles will be full of questions."

Father let out a long sigh and they turned just as he opened his eyes. "Marcus, my boy. And Alexandra. I thought you were at the front putting down the native rebellion."

"Thank The One God." Marcus leaned down and kissed Father's forehead. "We feared we'd lost you for a time."

Father pushed himself up higher and Marcus hurried to place pillows behind his back to support him. "Maybe you'd best tell me everything. Starting with how long I've been in this bed."

"It's been over a month," Marcus said.

"A month!" Father stared as if expecting them to start laughing at the joke. "How?"

"Cordius mixed poison with your cure all. It kept you unconscious and near death." Marcus shook his head. "We nearly didn't figure it out in time."

"*We* didn't figure anything out," Alexandra said. "Joran did."

"True. He's a remarkable fellow. To my shame, I trusted Cordius totally. If Alexandra and her advisor hadn't returned when they did, I might have stood by and let the traitor kill you. I'm so sorry, Father."

"Don't be. Cordius has tended me for nearly fifty years and never given me cause to doubt his loyalty. Why that changed, I can't imagine."

"No need to imagine," Alexandra said. "Some lunatic cult threatened to murder his granddaughter if he didn't kill you. Much as I wanted to hurt him, it's hard to fault a man for looking after his family first. Anyway, he's dead and we've nearly finished searching the palace for traitors."

Father rubbed the bridge of his nose. "It seems I've missed a great deal. Why don't you tell me everything?"

"There's rather a lot, Father," Marcus said. "Perhaps you should rest more."

"Bah! I've been resting too much as it is. Get me some food and start talking."

Alexandra smiled as she walked to the door. He sounded like himself again. That more than anything convinced her that Father had made a full recovery.

As soon as she sent a guard for food she returned to her father's bedside. She went first, detailing the explosion, her rescue, and the campaign to bring Stello Province under control. His eyes widened when she described the serpent, but otherwise he made no reaction until she finished.

Marcus took his turn, mostly focusing on the nobles and their concern for his heath.

Father barked a laugh at that. "Those vipers only care about my health insofar as it or my death will profit them. It seems the empire owes Joran Den Cade a great debt. I'll have to see him."

"I thought you'd want to." Alexandra went to the door again. When she opened it she turned to Joran and Mia and waved. "He wishes to speak with you."

Joran's expression made her smile. He looked a bit like a man on his way to the gallows. No doubt Father would quickly set his fears at ease. After all Joran had done, the last person he had to fear was the emperor.

————

Joran swallowed the lump in his throat and smoothed the front of his formal advisor's robe. Alexandra stood in the doorway waiting to introduce them to her father. Her father the emperor. As in the most powerful man in the world. He tried to swallow a second lump and found his mouth too dry. He had to get a hold of himself. Throwing up all over the emperor would not make a good first impression.

Mia laid a hand on his shoulder and his emotions steadied at once. "Remember, we fought a giant, imperial-steel-resistant serpent and won. You can handle an interview."

"Right. Thanks." He covered her hand with his for a moment then led the way over to the waiting princess. "Is he well?"

"Yes, your cure all has him back in perfect health. Though he seems a bit weak. I'm sure that's just a function of having lain in bed for a month. Come on. Father's anxious to meet you both."

They entered and Mia closed the door behind them. The bedroom looked exactly as Joran remembered from his last visit and Marcus looked considerably worse. Not that anyone save perhaps the emperor himself and doubtless Alexandra would dare point that out.

Speaking of the emperor, he sat in bed propped up by a mound of pillows. His color looked good and his dark eyes were open and bright. Forcing himself to look at the emperor as a patient and not a ruler helped Joran stay calm.

At the foot of the bed, he and Mia each took a knee and lowered their heads.

"An honor to meet you, Your Imperial Majesty," Joran said.

"Please stand and look at me," the emperor said. "My children have informed me of the many heroic deeds the two of you have performed on the empire's behalf. I wish to thank you personally for everything, not the least of which is saving my life."

Joran tried to command his knees not to wobble as he stood and failed miserably. "It was our honor to serve. Any citizen would have done the same were it in their power."

The emperor laughed, a deep, booming baritone that gave Joran a hint of what he'd sound like once he fully recovered. "If you believe that you're either an idiot, haven't met many members of the nobility, or are trying to be polite. People are always being polite to me. It comes with the job. Alexandra says you've been a good advisor, offering wise advice even when she wanted to hear something else. Whenever we speak, I need you to act the same way with me. There are plenty of people who will tell me what I want to hear. Including my dear children occasionally."

The lump grew again but Joran managed to speak. "If that is your command, I will, of course, do my best to comply."

"Good. Given all you've seen, what is the state of my empire?"

Joran licked his lips. "Precarious, Your Imperial Majesty. Many enemies, both within and without, conspire to destroy us. Those enemies need to be dealt with as quickly as possible lest they find some weapon even more dangerous than the serpent. I shudder to think what that might be, but I refuse to think it doesn't exist."

The emperor nodded. "I've thought much along those same lines. I will be counting on you to deal with these threats. There are few enough reliable people in the empire. Now, my son has promised you a reward for all you've done. Ask, and if it's within my power to grant, it's yours."

Joran truly only wanted one thing and given the situation he couldn't have it. "The empire has been beyond generous to my family. I want for nothing material. My only desire is to see the empire strong and safe. If it falls, the Den Cade family will lose everything. We are of imperial blood and would be hunted anywhere we went. I need no reward and swear on my honor as a citizen that I will do all I can to keep the empire from falling."

The emperor's smile held a warmth Joran wouldn't have believed possible. "That is the most honorable sentiment I have ever heard a nobleman express that I actually believed. I didn't know that I was looking for you, Joran. May I call you by your given name?"

Joran tried not to grin and failed. The emperor was turning out to be nothing like what he expected. His nerves felt steady now. Amazing what you could get used to.

"You may call me anything you wish, Your Imperial Majesty."

"Splendid. In that case, I will choose a reward for you. You shall marry my daughter."

A blast of pleasure so powerful he nearly fainted ran through Joran. Of all Mia's potential reactions, he hadn't expected that one. For his part, Joran struggled to keep his expression smooth even as he considered the implications of marrying into the imperial family. Keeping his focus strategic rather than personal helped steady him.

A few feet away, Alexandra's jaw dropped. "What?"

"He will be a good match for you and having someone loyal to the empire join our family will make us stronger. At the very least we won't have to rely on someone outside the family should one of us get sick. And given the work you must do, both, no, all three of you must act with my full favor. No one can doubt you move at my command and with my trust. What better way to show that than to grant Joran the greatest treasure in the empire?"

Alexandra's cheeks flushed. "But, I thought... I mean, I thought you were waiting to find me a husband that would serve some greater diplomatic cause. No offense to Joran, but the Den Cade family are merchants and minor nobles with no particular alliances with the great houses or military. How does my marrying him further our diplomatic goals?"

"It doesn't." The emperor chuckled. "Did you really think the reason I hadn't chosen you a husband was diplomatic? I hoped to find someone honorable, that wouldn't use you to gain power or worse get close enough to kill me and Marcus before trying to seize the throne. Don't doubt for a moment that there are those among the nobility that would think nothing of killing us all if it served their goals. Everything Joran has done and said tells me he's the man I've sought. Do you disagree? Of all present you've spent the most time with him."

Joran wasn't sure he wanted to hear her answer.

"No, I don't disagree. He's saved my life twice and put his on the line while asking for nothing in return. If I must marry, I could certainly do worse."

"Good, that's settled," the emperor said, without asking if Joran wanted to marry Alexandra. "Now for Mia."

"Me, Your Imperial Majesty?" She crept up closer to stand beside Joran.

"Indeed. If you are to continue your good works with your soulmate, it's necessary for you to become a member of the nobility. Otherwise, eventually some idiot will claim you have no right to go somewhere you need to go."

"I would be honored for my family to adopt Mia," Joran said. "I already have two brothers; a sister would be welcome."

"Noble? Me?" Mia looked at Joran with tears glistening in her eyes. "You would have me for a sister? A commoner with no family and nothing to offer?"

"Without a moment's hesitation. You are already my soul's twin. Why not be my sister in the eyes of the law as well?"

She hugged him and the emperor cleared his throat.

They immediately broke apart. "Forgive us, Your Imperial Majesty," Joran said.

"No need to apologize. You two have warmed my cynical

heart. And if you are to marry my daughter, then you must call me Father as well, at least in private. I'll also write an imperial request should your parents prove less enthusiastic about adopting Mia than you are."

"One small thing, Father." Joran couldn't believe he'd said that without stammering. He did draw a glare from Alexandra which brought a smirk from Marcus. "Would it be possible for me to tell my parents all this before you make a formal announcement? I don't want them to collapse when they get the news."

The emperor chuckled again. "Good idea. Take Alexandra home for dinner and to meet them. Nothing like having a member of the imperial family in your dining room to encourage the right thinking. I'll have the letter ready for you tomorrow. I think a spring wedding would be nice, don't you?"

Joran nodded as if marrying into the imperial family were no big deal while his mind raced to figure out what this all meant for his future and his family's.

Alexandra said, "If that's your wish, Father."

Someone knocked and a muffled voice said, "The food is here, Your Imperial Majesty."

"Perfect timing," the emperor said. "You three run along and make your plans. I believe a meal and a nap will suit me very well."

Joran and Mia bowed and Alexandra led the way out. The guards all saluted as they passed. They made the walk back to Alexandra's suite in silence and not until they were inside and the servants dismissed did Alexandra turn and glare at him.

"What?" Joran asked. "This wasn't my idea. I couldn't have been more surprised."

"It's nice that your father took your happiness and not just politics into consideration," Mia dared suggest.

"It is," Alexandra said at last. "It's also nice that Ventor will be annoyed that he can't marry me himself now. But I suppose I'll have to have a couple kids and hang around the palace instead of leading the army. I can't imagine anything more tedious. I don't know how Marcus's wife stands it."

"Kids won't be a problem," Joran said. "I probably should have mentioned this sooner, but I can't father children."

Both Mia's and Alexandra's gazes shifted to his crotch.

"No, that works just fine. Overexposure to a certain chemical damaged whatever it is that lets you reproduce. A cure all can't repair the damage since it's more of a curse than an injury or disease. I knew the risks, but I needed that particular chemical for the experiment I was running. I figured even if the worst happened, Titus already had a son at the time, so he could carry on the Den Cade name. Besides, I'm too distracted to make a good father. I'm sure your father will call off the wedding if you explain the situation to him."

"Are you kidding?" Alexandra asked. "This is perfect. No kids means I can keep fighting. Like you, my brother has two sons. That's plenty of spare heirs."

She actually looked excited at the prospect of marrying him now. The reasons kind of disappointed him, but if he was stuck marrying her, better for him if the prospect pleased her.

"I need to change. The investigation team will arrive today. You can vet them and I'll give them their assignment." She practically skipped to her bedroom.

"She seems happy," Mia said.

"Yeah. Speaking of that, why were you so excited when the emperor announced his plan? I figured you'd hate me for ending up with the one you loved."

"I could never hate you and Alexandra will never love me, I understand that now. But thanks to our soul bond, when you have sex with her, it will be like I'm doing it too. I'll feel everything. How amazing will that be?"

Joran had read about voyeurism, though this sounded extreme. But it must be the same for other soulmates. Oddly, the prospect of sharing even that most intimate of acts with Mia didn't really trouble him. Since he assumed Alexandra understood how a soul bond worked and she'd said nothing about it, she must have been okay with it as well. Of course, if she wasn't, there was nothing Joran could do. Only death could break a soul bond.

He just hoped he didn't disappoint either of them.

CHAPTER 10

A horrible smell filled the air. Lovia had no idea what caused it, but every time they came to speak with the overseer, it made her nose hairs burn. The overseer sat in what she thought of as his throne, really just a black leather chair lit by a single alchemical lamp directly overhead. It cast a long shadow across his face, obscuring his features. He wore a dark, loose-fitting tunic and trousers as well as black leather gloves. Everything about him suggested a lack of trust in his subordinates..

Or perhaps she was reading too much into it. After all, if one of the members didn't know what he looked like, they couldn't tell anyone should they be caught. Deep shadows obscured the rest of the room. If someone had asked Lovia where the magic took her, she wouldn't have had an answer.

Her partner, Thomison, completed his report. He'd held nothing back and made no effort to paint their failure in a more flattering light. Lovia knew little enough about the overseer, but thought it would have done no harm to push some of the blame, or perhaps most of it, onto their enemies.

The overseer steepled his fingers and leaned back. His entire face vanished in the darkness. "So, the plan is a total failure, your cell is reduced to just the two of you, and all our agents have been forced to flee the palace or risk discovery. We are now completely blind to the emperor's plans. Did I leave anything out?"

Thomison said nothing, but Lovia refused to shoulder all the blame. "We did the best we could. Grandfather would have completed the mission had Joran Den Cade not shown up when he did. It's his fault, not ours."

"No," the overseer said. "When you are given a mission, succeed or fail, the results are your responsibility. If a new challenge pops up, you must surmount it. That is the way of The One True God. Those hypocrites in the church might say that divine will meant their god didn't want them to succeed and so they didn't. We know better. Higher powers care nothing for us. Our own efforts and nothing else decide our fate."

Lovia stared. How could they overcome a challenge they didn't anticipate? They'd have to be fortune tellers able to see the future. It was an impossible standard.

"Do not think I am immune to our rules," the overseer said. "If enough of my teams fail, the archbishop will call me to answer for my own failures. And I assure you, blaming my teams' incompetence will do nothing to lessen her wrath. I create and oversee the teams; therefore your failures reflect my poor choices."

"How do we make it right?" Thomison asked.

"Your partner, despite her desire to deflect responsibility away from the two of you, isn't incorrect about Joran Den Cade. He needs to understand that a price must be paid for opposing us. You will kill his father and bring his mother to me. Should he wish her to live, he will need to obey us. We've lost one alchemist and healer; a replacement will be necessary. Do this, and your earlier failure will be forgiven. Better you die trying than return here again in defeat."

Lovia swallowed hard. She'd never killed anyone. She'd never even swung a sword. Even with Thomison's powers, it seemed an impossible task.

"May we hire help?" Thomison asked.

"If you have funds, use them how you feel best," the overseer said. "I care not in the least how you accomplish the task, so long as it is done. Go now and complete your mission in The One True God's name."

Thomison bowed and Lovia quickly followed suit. They turned and at the very edge of the room a new light flared to life, a glowing circle of strange markings. Lovia read and spoke several languages, but she'd never seen marks like these before.

They stepped into the circle and after an instant of pain that felt like she was being torn apart, the light vanished. They found themselves in the basement of the cult's primary base in Tiber surrounded by a different circle of markings similar to the ones in the overseer's chamber.

Thomison led the way out and as they went upstairs, she asked, "How are we going to do what he wants? I'm no fighter."

"There is no shortage of men willing to kill for money and I have plenty saved. We can hire a dozen fighters, and along with my magic, taking the Den Cades will be no problem."

"How can you be so sure?"

"I've been by their home. They keep no guards, only servants. The arrogant fools doubtless believe themselves safe in Tiber's Third Circle, surrounded by wealth and luxury. We will teach them the error of their ways and save our own hides in the process."

Lovia found her mouth too dry to swallow. She loved Thomison, but his dark side gave her chills. "How can I help?"

"When the time comes, I'll need you by my side. The magic leaves me vulnerable. Having you on lookout will free me to act as necessary."

At the top of the stairs, she wrapped her arms around him. "I'm with you to the end. Whatever happens."

Thomison covered her hand with his, the warmth of his grasp spreading through her. They would be okay. Lovia knew it.

———

J orik sat in his office and read the message scroll Titus sent. Apparently, negotiations with the dwarves were taking longer than expected. An agent from Den March trading had arrived and now Titus had them to bid against. Not ideal and it would drive up the cost of acquiring the new mineral, but if Titus secured exclusive rights to distribute it in the empire, they stood to more than recoup their costs. On the negative side, it looked like Titus would have to spend the winter with the dwarves.

He needed Joran back and he needed him back now. Contract or not, his youngest would have to step up and help run the business. Either that or Jorik needed to find a couple more reliable managers. Easier said than done considering the failure at his trading post in Cularo.

Someone knocked and said, "Message, my lord."

Jorik stood, his back and knees cracking, and walked to the door. The house footman waited with another rolled-up scroll. Not from Titus. The last one only arrived three days ago.

"Did it come by coach?" Jorik took the scroll and smiled at the stylized J on the seal. Joran at last.

"No, my lord, a runner in palace livery showed up at the front door just this moment."

Jorik's smile withered. What had that boy gotten himself into? Nothing good ever came from dealing with the imperial family. They hated to pay and Jorik's meager title didn't impress them in the least.

"Is there anything else, my lord?" the footman asked.

Jorik had forgotten the man still waited. "No, thank you."

He bowed and withdrew. Jorik closed the door and unrolled the scroll. The brief message indicated that Joran had returned from Stello Province, the trading post was a total loss, and he'd taken up the position of Princess Alexandra's personal advisor. No details beyond a request to have dinner and that he had two lady friends he wanted to introduce to the family.

None of that was fantastic news, though if Joran had finally found a woman to settle down with, Sestia would be pleased. He doubted it was that. Otherwise, he would have said only one lady friend. So many questions and so few answers.

He rolled the scroll back up and stepped out into the hall. He'd completely lost track of time but guessed it was late afternoon. Making his silent way along the thick carpet, he headed for the back garden. Sestia liked to putter out there this time of day and Jorik hadn't heard it raining.

A couple turns brought him to a sliding wood-and-paper door. Outside he spotted his wife only a few feet into the sprawling garden. She wore a simple white tunic and leggings with her sandals. Sestia knelt in front of a flower bed surrounded by a foot-high wall made of small stones and worked with a knife to divide bulbs. At least that's what he thought she was doing. There were dozens of such beds scattered throughout the garden, all tended by a small staff of gardeners, plus Sestia when she felt like some fresh air. He preferred to spend his garden time sitting in the shade sipping wine.

He closed the door a little louder than necessary and she turned, ready to correct a servant. Instead, she smiled, dropped her knife, and walked over to him. "This is a surprise. I figured you'd be working for at least another hour."

"I got a message from Joran."

She lit up like the sun. "Is he alright?"

"Fine and back in Tiber." He handed Sestia the note.

She read it then looked up at him. "Kind of vague. Day after tomorrow is our regular dinner night, want to invite him and his mystery women? Camellia and the boys are coming as well. We can introduce everyone."

"Fine with me. I'm less interested in the women than what happened to my trading post. He was supposed to fire the manager and promote the assistant. How in the world do you go from that to a total loss?"

"As long as he's safe, we can afford to lose a trading post." Sestia brushed past him and hurried into the house. She called back over her shoulder. "I'll have the cook arrange the ingredients to prepare his favorite stew."

Jorik's mouth watered. That was his favorite too. And she had a point. No doubt Joran had faced some danger on his trip south. Hopefully the journey had given him a real taste for adventure. But even if it hadn't, as long as he'd come home safe, nothing else really mattered.

———

Quintus Den Cade undid his pants and drained his bladder onto the side of the cheap, First Circle tavern. From the smell of it, he wasn't the first one to do so. A shake and a tuck had him ready for a refill. He loved drinking in this part of the city. No one knew him, so his father wouldn't get a report about his evening's entertainment.

Not that he thought Father really cared anymore. That actually hurt worse than the lectures he used to get. He didn't know how Joran stood listening to Father rattle on about adventure and the proper manners for a man. Titus, at least, seemed to fully embrace the family legacy. "The good son" they called him and not without reason.

He groaned, shook his head, and scratched the stubble

covering his cheeks. He needed a shave badly and a bath worse. Nothing like a four-day debauch to mess up your outfit. With the allowance Father gave him, he could afford to simply trash the ruined tunic and trousers and buy new ones. Of course, that would cut into his drinking money.

He shook his head again. So many problems.

Quintus stumbled a step and caught himself on the wall. The bad thing about drinking in this part of the city was that no one knew where he lived, so getting carried back to his apartment would be a problem. Maybe he'd just pick up a bottle and finish it at home. Assuming he made the walk without ending up on the side of the street passed out. He'd done it before of course, but that didn't mean Quintus enjoyed sleeping outdoors. Autumn had come and the nights were properly chilly.

Maybe he'd better swing by a particular street corner and pick up some company for the evening. If he found his favorite girl, she'd tumble him for half the bottle. A bargain at twice the price.

Grinning, he pushed away from the wall and staggered off at a determined shuffle.

He ambled a few blocks before a voice caught his attention. Pausing to listen, he frowned. Why had that voice broken through the haze? Very little usually did that.

"We're hitting Den Cade Manor," the voice said again. "The deal is we get paid and we can take whatever we can carry. You'll be rich."

Quintus found his pleasant inebriation washed away in a tide of panic. Someone planned to rob the manor. That sounded insane, but then again, as long as they got into the Third Circle, the family kept no guards on the grounds. The servants certainly wouldn't last long against armed thugs.

He moved closer to the alley where he heard the voice. A rough-looking man in leathers armed with a shortsword on his hip spoke with another man who sat against the wall. Quintus had met some rough characters during his nightly wandering, but these looked about the worst.

The fellow on his feet must have noticed Quintus as he turned and reached for the hilt of his sword. "Piss off, mate."

"I heard your offer," Quintus said before he could think better of it. "If you want swords, I'm your man."

"I don't know you." The swordsman stepped closer. "And you don't look like much of a fighter."

"That's because I'm out drinking, not looking for a duel. If there's a battle, you'll be glad to have me along. No offense to the fellow you were trying to recruit, but he appears to have died."

The derelict had in fact fallen over on his side, but loud snores indicated that he hadn't, in fact, expired.

"Useless idiot." The swordsman turned back and shot Quintus a hard look. "Alright. Meet us at Rose Park in Second Circle at seven bells the night after next. And bring a damn sword."

The swordsman stalked off, no doubt to interview another bum about murder.

Quintus hurried away, his plans for the rest of the night forgotten. He was a bit hazy on the date, but felt quite certain that two nights hence was family dinner night. Drunk though he might be, he had no intention of letting his family be killed.

CHAPTER 11

Jorik paced near the front door, smoothed his beard, and paced some more. He didn't even know why he felt nervous. Camellia and the boys had arrived a few minutes ago and Joran should be here soon. Maybe the fact that his youngest son had never brought a girl home to meet them and now he was bringing two. Jorik hardly considered himself a prude, but polygamy, while not illegal, would raise eyebrows. He had a few clients, extremely wealthy and influential clients, with very particular opinions on that sort of thing and feared they might take their business to Den March Trading should they find out.

Assuming he hadn't asked to bring the women for some other reason. Jorik tried his best to imagine what that might be and failed.

"Will you calm down?" Sestia emerged from the dining room where she'd been playing with the boys. She wore her favorite blue robe, the one colored with Joran's dye. "When he gets here everything will be explained and your fretting won't speed that in the least."

Jorik stopped and a moment later heard footsteps outside. They were here.

The door opened and the footman said, "Joran Den Cade, Mia Amino, and Her Majesty Alexandra Tiberius."

Jorik's jaw nearly hit the floor. The first woman's name meant nothing to him, but the second everyone in the empire recognized. The Iron Princess. Joran had brought the Iron Princess to dinner.

As soon as the footman completed his announcement, Joran led the way into the entry hall. He wore a fine robe of crimson and silver and around his neck hung a platinum amulet engraved with the imperial eagle clutching a sword in its talons: Princess Alexandra's personal symbol.

Immediately behind Joran had to be Mia Amino, a slim, muscular woman about his son's age. Her eyes held the hard, wary look he'd long come to associate with warriors. Her uncomfortable movements argued unfamiliarity with her formal crimson robes. Though clearly an imperial, Jorik guessed she was of common blood. Why had he brought a commoner along with the princess?

Speaking of Her Majesty, Princess Alexandra brought up the rear of the group. She dressed in a crimson and silver robe that matched Joran's but left her legs bare below the knee. Her short hair had been perfectly combed and her makeup looked flawless. The half-ancient slaves might have been more beautiful, but other than them, Jorik couldn't think of anyone else that came close.

"Father, Mother," Joran said. "Allow me to introduce you to Mia Amino, my soulmate. And I'm sure you recognize my fiancée, Princess Alexandra."

Jorik's mouth worked but no sound emerged. Joran had found his soulmate and gotten engaged to the imperial princess? He'd only been gone for about two months. How did all that happen?

Lucky for him Sestia's brain still functioned properly. "Your Majesty, welcome to our humble home. It is a great honor to have you and an even greater honor to learn that you will be joining our family."

"Thank you," the princess said. "Joran has been a great help to the imperial family, even saving my life twice. Father deemed our marriage good for the empire and for the two of us. The official announcement won't be for another week, but Joran insisted that we meet face-to-face beforehand."

The princess held out her hand and Sestia took it gently. "My other daughter-in-law is in the dining room with my grandsons. You'll have to meet them."

"Mother," Joran said. "Don't be rude to my other guest. Mia and I share a soul after all."

"Of course." Sestia tore her gaze away from the princess and moved closer to Mia. "Pleasure to meet you, dear."

A quick handshake and she hurried back to lead the princess toward the dining room.

Jorik caught his son mutter, "Don't take it personally. Mother can't help herself."

Mia shrugged and smiled as if untroubled by Sestia's behavior. Jorik finally pulled himself together and joined them.

"You've been busy, son."

"You have no idea, Father. Wait until I tell you the whole story."

——————

Quintus arrived at Rose Park just as seven bells rang out. He doubted Father would believe him capable of arriving anywhere on time, but when you're trying to thwart the murder of your family, timeliness was essential. Along with sobriety. His head pounded from the hangover, but not nearly as bad as yesterday. He doubted he'd been sober this long since he was a boy.

About half a block square, the park had a handful of granite benches along with a small garden that needed some serious attention before the weeds fully took over. There must have been a few roses mixed in as the smell of them filled the air.

Adjusting his broadsword, Quintus strode into the park with a swagger appropriate for the part he played. A dozen other armed men had already arrived, including the swordsman that had recruited him the other night.

The swordsman met him a little ways from the main group. "I'm impressed. Figured you were all talk. Two of my regulars didn't show, so I'm glad to be wrong. Name's Patronix, welcome to the party."

Patronix thrust his hand out and Quintus shook it. "Quin, and I love a good party. When do we get started?"

"As soon as the boss gets here."

Quintus frowned. "Thought you were the boss."

Patronix barked a laugh. "Not for a job this big. I'm more of a centurion, though we're far short of a full century. The boss hired me to find you and the others."

"He must trust you."

Patronix shrugged. "Not a lot of people that do what I do. You want muscle on short notice, no questions asked, I'm your man. Anyway, shouldn't be long now. Come on."

They joined the other fighters, all of them dressed in ragged leathers and stinking fouler than Quintus on his worst night. Weapons varied from man to man, but all of them had more than one. Quintus felt a bit underequipped, but tried not to let his discomfort show.

A five-minute wait brought the arrival of a man and woman, both dressed in dark, hooded cloaks that disguised their features. Quintus hadn't expected to know them and people plotting the murder of a prominent family wouldn't exactly advertise their identity.

The man waved Patronix over and a rather animated conversation took place in hushed voices. The other mercenaries started muttering among themselves. Whatever happened, they hadn't expected it. Good sign or bad, he had yet to decide.

Finally, Patronix nodded and turned to face them. "Well, men, there's been a complication. It seems three new targets have shown up along with a force of guards. Our employer says he can deal with the guards, but the situation isn't what I promised you. Anyone wants out, now's the time to speak."

More muttering and shared dark looks. Greed and caution warred in the men's expressions.

More curious than anything, Quintus asked, "Who showed up?"

"The youngest son along with Princess Alexandra and a second, unknown woman. The guards are Iron Legion elite. But as I said, our employer says he can deal with them. A whelp and two women. You're not going to let those three stand in the way of your loot, are you?"

"Hell no!" someone shouted and soon the call was taken up by the others. Sounded like they'd found their enthusiasm.

For his part, Quintus actually felt a little better knowing Joran had arrived for the family dinner. His little brother might not be much of a fighter, but if he brought any of his alchemy tricks, that would even the odds considerably.

"Then let's go!" Patronix waved a hand and they marched toward the nearby gate to Third Circle. How a dozen thugs would sneak past the guards on duty, Quintus had no idea.

The answer became apparent when they arrived. The guardhouse and wall above appeared abandoned. A quick look left and right confirmed no patrols in sight.

How had they managed that?

Quintus found his curiosity piqued by the mystery duo. They had to have some serious connections to clear this entire sector.

The group sprinted through, quickly putting the gate behind them. Den Cade Manor sat only a few blocks from the gate and soon enough they stopped again. From a distance, the squad of Iron Guards were readily visible standing in the light of two alchemical lamps near the manor's ten-foot-tall iron fence.

Patronix held a finger to his lips.

The boss and his lady friend moved a little bit apart from the group. The woman pulled a vial out of the folds of her cloak. Quintus had seen enough of them to recognize an alchemical weapon of some sort.

The man raised his hands and the vial lifted out of the woman's grasp and flew through the darkening sky. Quintus had certainly never seen that before.

When the vial reached a point directly above the guards, it tipped upside down and powder fell gently down over them. One by one the guards collapsed and after a minute they had a clear path.

"Let's go," Patronix said in a fierce whisper.

The fighters all drew their weapons. Quintus followed suit and then they were off. Not exactly how he expected his first visit home in four years to go.

CHAPTER 12

Joran finished the last of his stew and sighed. He'd missed the food if not the stress of family dinner. Titus's boys got as much on their faces as they did in their mouths, though Sextus had improved a great deal from the last time Joran ate with them. Alexandra shot the kids a look of disgust, but Mia seemed genuinely amused.

The princess might not think much of the boys' table manners, but she seemed to enjoy the food. Her plate ended up as clean as Joran's own. Mia's too for that matter, though Joran had never seen her leave any food behind whatever they ate.

When the slaves came to take away the plates, Camellia took the opportunity to haul the boys off to the washroom to clean them up.

"I hope you liked the food, Majesty," Mother said.

"It was delicious, thank you. And call me Alexandra. We'll all be family soon enough. Once the engagement is made official, you'll have to come to the palace so we can repay your generosity."

Mother's smile brightened the room. "We'd be delighted of course."

Father offered a sour smile of his own. He'd never had much of a taste for fancy dinners, though he did attend them for business reasons. He took a sip of wine. "When do you think it will be safe to resume trading in Stello Province?"

"Any time you want," Alexandra said. "We have a peace treaty with the natives now, so it should be calm enough."

"Have your agent find Draq and tell him I sent you," Joran added. "You should have no trouble making a deal with his tribe. I told him you'd be fair, so please don't make a liar out of me."

"I'm fair with all my partners," Father said.

"Of course you are, but I know some of your agents can be a little aggressive during negotiations. Please remind whoever you send not to screw up what little goodwill we've accumulated."

"I'll mention it." Father leaned forward in his seat. "Unless you want to handle the negotiations."

"Joran has more important work that requires his full attention," Alexandra said in the tone imperial family members had that made it clear the topic was closed. For the first time, Joran actually appreciated it.

"Well," Mother said. "Shall we retire to the sitting room? I'd love to hear more about how you two came to fall in love."

Alexandra looked at Joran who smiled and shook his head. "In love" didn't exactly describe their relationship. Mutual respect, certainly, maybe even friendship, but love? No, he didn't love her. And he seriously doubted she loved him. In time, perhaps, but given who and what she was, Joran doubted Alexandra would allow herself to love anyone fully. Not that he considered himself a romantic either.

Mia tugged his sleeve and whispered, "I hear footsteps outside. The heavy tread of men running. I told you I should have brought a sword."

Joran grimaced. Trouble always seemed to find them, even

in Tiber's Third Circle. He'd assumed no one would dare do anything here.

Stupid idea. If the cult had guts enough to try and poison the emperor, attacking Joran's home would be no leap.

"We're about to have company," Joran announced. "My assumption is that they are violent, armed men that wish to kill us all. Father, do you still have those swords in the study?"

"Yes, but they're mostly for decoration. I don't think they're even sharp."

Mia picked up her steak knife, held it like a fighting dagger and leapt to her feet. "They're getting closer."

"What's this all about?" Mother asked.

"I fear my troubles have followed me home." Joran stood and Alexandra joined him.

He slipped a vial of paralyzing powder into his hand. He no longer went anywhere unarmed. He'd prefer to use dread spores to thin out the attackers, but didn't dare risk it with so many people he didn't want to hurt around.

A crash and shout from the entry hall made it clear their time for planning had ended.

"Forget the swords," Joran said. "Let's get to your office. We can barricade the door, that will buy us some time. Get Camellia and the boys and let's go."

Camellia chose that moment to return, her now neatly scrubbed children in tow. She looked past the table and screamed.

Mia whipped her knife forward, drawing a gurgling moan.

One down and who knew how many to go.

Joran grabbed the edge of the table and Mia got the other side. No need to share his plan; she knew his intentions as soon as he thought them. Together they heaved the heavy table at the gang of men rushing down the hall toward the dining room.

It crashed into the front pair, staggering them back into the rest.

That wouldn't buy much time.

The group ran for Father's office. Ten feet from the dining room they turned down a narrow hall, Father and Mother in the lead. Mia brought up the rear, a second knife in her hand.

Joran nearly ran his father over when he stopped. Beyond him two men blocked their passage.

"Quintus?" Joran barely got the question out before his eldest brother ran the second man through the back.

Quintus waved at them. "Come on, we can get out through the garden."

They needed no further convincing. Mia paused to swap her knife for the dead man's sword and slit the sides of her fancy robe to make running easier. Joran felt considerably better having a fully armed Mia on their team.

The shouts and pounding footsteps behind them were less encouraging. He glanced back and hurled the vial at the right-hand wall. The burst of powder had to have hit a few of them judging from the thuds.

They reached the garden and found a semicircle of five men waiting. In the center stood two figures in concealing robes. The ringleaders no doubt.

Three more thugs emerged from the house behind them.

Joran pulled another vial, this one filled with acid. Maybe he'd get lucky and take out a couple more.

"Don't throw that," Quintus said. "The man in the robes can use some kind of magic to move objects."

Joran had never heard of such a thing and given Quintus's proclivities wondered if he'd hallucinated it. But he did seem fairly sober, so perhaps it would be best to give him the benefit of the doubt.

The attackers hesitated to attack, though Joran had no idea why. They had the advantage of numbers.

Remembering Quintus's warning, he looked up and spotted the vial floating toward them.

Clever. Let's see if the cultist could handle two at once.

Joran hurled the acid at the cloaked figure with all his might.

The acid deflected right, smashing into the ground. As soon as it did, the vial above them dropped. Joran caught it and breathed in a little of the powder inside. Sour, like lemons. Paralyzing powder for sure.

Lucky for him he was immune.

He spun and threw it at the men behind them.

The vial exploded, sending powder everywhere and dropping the men to the ground.

That evened the odds a little bit.

"Thanks for the warning, Quintus."

Alexandra straightened and glared at the remaining invaders. "What do you want?"

"Your lives," the cloaked man said.

The thugs surged forward. Mia and Quintus shifted to face them.

Quintus squared off against an older man armed with a shortsword and a dagger.

For her part, Mia moved like lightning, cutting down two of the thugs in the blink of an eye, before the other two switched to a defensive position and managed to deflect her attacks.

"I knew I shouldn't have trusted you," the man dueling Quintus said.

Joran had only half an ear for the conversation. His focus remained on the hooded cultists. One looked like a woman and neither of them showed any sign of joining the battle. Did they only know how to use magic? He had no idea, but didn't plan to get caught by surprise.

Alexandra coughed, gasped, and clawed at her throat as she struggled to breathe. So that was the plan. Joran bent and snatched a rock off the top of one of the planting bed walls. If alchemists knew anything combat related, it was how to throw accurately.

His hand snapped out and the rock raced across the garden, striking the hooded man in his shadowed face. He went over sideways and Alexandra took a deep breath.

The woman screamed. "Thomison!"

Mia chose that moment to gut one of her opponents. Without backup, the second one didn't last much longer.

A second, well-placed stone distracted the swordsman hacking at Quintus just enough for his brother to cut into the side of his neck.

When Joran turned his attention to the hooded woman, he found her gone. He grimaced, but didn't feel like complaining. That the whole family made it out alive seemed a minor miracle.

"Next time we're eating at the palace," Alexandra said.

"Sure," Joran said. "It's not like anyone's ever tried to kill us there."

"Not this many."

She had him there. The boys chose that moment to burst into tears. Camellia did her best to calm them, but running for your life and watching men get killed in front of you had to do something to a kid's psyche. With any luck, they'd get over it quickly.

"Anyone want to tell me what the hell is going on?" Father asked.

"I'd love to, Father, but first we need to get things tied up here. That paralyzing powder doesn't last forever and I doubt the guy I hit is dead. At least I hope he's not. We need information." Joran clapped his brother on the shoulder. "Excellent timing on your return to family dinners, Quintus."

Quintus grinned. "Seemed like a good idea. You've grown, Joran. And I don't mean in height. Last time I saw you, something like this would have sent you fleeing for your life. Now you take it in stride."

Joran smiled back. "I've had a lot of practice since then.

More than I'd like, to be honest. Can I ask you to take the family back inside? There must be some rope. Get Father to help you tie up any of the surviving mercenaries. We'll join you as soon as we finish with this bunch."

"No problem. Besides, I need a drink."

Joran's eyes narrowed in disappointment. Same old Quintus after all. When his brother had fought to save them, he'd dared hope for something more.

With his family out of sight Joran blew out a long sigh. "Are you both okay?"

Through their link, he knew Mia hadn't been hurt in the fight. Alexandra worried him more, but he didn't want to single her out for extra attention.

"I'm fine," Mia said. "I've fought more pathetic warriors, but not in some time. How did they get past the Iron Guards out front?"

"I suspect a combination of paralyzing powder and that man's magic." Joran stepped over a body and led the way over to the cloaked figure. As he'd hoped, the man still breathed.

"Run around and check on those idiots," Alexandra said.

"Yes, Majesty." Mia ran out of the garden and around toward the front of the house.

Alexandra kicked the unconscious man onto his back with a good deal more force than necessary. "I've never felt anything like what he did to me. Try as I might, the air wouldn't go into my lungs. I thought I was going to die."

Joran squeezed her shoulder. "But you didn't."

"Thanks to you, again." Alexandra grabbed the front of his tunic, pulled him close, and kissed him hard on the lips.

Joran cleared his throat. "My pleasure. In the meantime, does the name Thomison mean anything to you?"

She shook her head. "I suspect they're all commoners, and some of the mercenaries look like provincials. Outside of the army and the palace servants, I don't deal with commoners."

"I do, but I don't know this one. Much as I want to question him, with no way to control his magic, I'm tempted to simply kill him right now while we can."

Mia came running around the corner into the garden. Her face looked flushed though he suspected the kiss he shared with Alexandra had more to do with it than the short run. "The guards are fine, though still frozen stiff as boards. I didn't know what else to do, so I left them where they were."

"There won't be any traffic through this part of the city until midmorning, so they should be fine. The powder only lasts an hour anyway." Joran stretched and yawned. The adrenaline had started to wear off and he felt exhausted.

"Kill him," Alexandra said at last. "Whatever he knows isn't worth the risk."

Without a moment's hesitation Mia raised her borrowed sword and hacked Thomison's head off with a single powerful strike.

Good thing Joran suggested taking the kids inside.

"Can you spare a century of Iron Legionnaires?" Joran asked. "There's no way I can leave the manor unprotected after this."

"Most of the Iron Legion is still in Stello Province. But I'll do you one better. We'll borrow a century from the First. That will show that your family is under Father's personal protection. Only a genuine madman would risk taking them on, magic or not."

"Thank you. While I doubt Thomison would be dumb enough to carry incriminating information on him, I think I'll search his body just to make sure. After that, I fear a long talk with Mother and Father will be necessary. Will it be alright if I tell them everything?"

"After tonight, I think you'd better."

They barely got the last mercenary tied up before the powder started to wear off. Joran badly wanted to sleep, but the look on his parents' faces made it clear explanations wouldn't wait for another day. Camellia and the boys had decided to stay the night and were resting in one of the unused rooms deeper in the house away from the lingering smell of blood. Some of the servants were busy trying to scrub the entry hall clean, but Joran suspected the stink would linger.

When they checked for survivors, he'd felt sick at the sight of the family footman lying in a pool of blood. The old man had been with them since before Joran was born and he hadn't even known the man's name. Though he thought of himself as a man of the people, he'd never thought to ask about the footman's family. No doubt the proper fellow would have been scandalized by someone of Joran's rank asking him such things, but still he wished he had.

As least Quintus had limited himself to a single shot of brandy to take the edge off. Father had drained two himself and so had no right to criticize.

"If we're going to talk," Joran said. "Let's go to the sitting room. This area is a mess."

"What about them?" Mother shot a disdainful look at the slowly recovering mercenaries.

"We'll take them to the palace when we leave," Alexandra said. "They'll be questioned before execution."

"Good." Mother led the way down a short hall to the sitting room. Enough comfortable seats for twice their number filled the room.

Joran settled in the middle of an overstuffed couch with Mia and Alexandra on either side of him. The rest of the family sat in leather chairs opposite them. Joran took a deep breath and laid it all out, from the moment he boarded the carriage south until just before arriving for dinner. Mia and Alexandra chimed in occasionally, but seemed content to let him do most of the talking.

For their part, his parents just stared in dumbstruck horror. Mother gasped when he described the serpent though Father seemed more upset at the news that Den March Trading had bought off one of his employees.

"So now you know everything," Joran said. "There's an insane cult dedicated to destroying the empire. I fear I've now done enough to draw their attention. Which means you all will be in danger. I hope you won't argue about the guards Alexandra offered."

"We won't," Father said. "And I'm sorry, son. When I sent you on that trip, I never imagined it would turn out the way it did. I never intended to put you in such danger. I just wanted you to see more of the world."

"I know, Father. And regardless of what happened, I wouldn't trade finding Mia for anything. I wish you could know the joy that comes from finding your soulmate. It's a joy beyond anything I can imagine." Mia's pleasure washed over him and he knew she felt the same without her saying a word. "Alexandra has been remarkable in her own way as well. I may well be the luckiest man in the world despite everything else that happened."

"Speaking of lucky." Father turned to Quintus. "What about you?"

Quintus told his tale, no doubt glossing over some of the less-flattering details. "I figured having a man on the inside would give you a better chance to escape. And, frankly, I doubted you'd believe me if I sent a warning note."

"Would you blame me if I didn't?" Father asked.

Before an argument had a chance to erupt, Mother put a hand on Father's arm. "Quintus is here now and he saved us all. That's what matters."

Father blew out a long breath. "It certainly is. Thank you, son."

After a moment of stunned silence Quintus grinned. "My pleasure."

"Will you stay at the manor for a while?" Joran asked. "You may be a target now as well."

Quintus's grin shriveled. "You know how to kill the moment, little brother. I'll stay, for a little while anyway."

"Camellia and the boys should as well," Mother said. "What about Titus?"

"I'll send him a letter," Father said. "Right now, he's probably safer with the dwarves than he would be here."

"Assuming The One True God cult doesn't have any followers among the dwarves." Everyone looked at Mia and she blushed. "Sorry."

"Don't be," Joran said. "You're quite right. Still, I think Father has a point. Hopefully we can have the capital secure before Titus returns in the spring."

"We'll have to wait until he gets back for the wedding," Alexandra said.

In all the excitement, Joran had forgotten the emperor had said they should have a spring wedding. It was strange that he felt mostly disconnected to the event that would make him part of the imperial family if only by marriage. He had no real control over that, so tried his best not to worry. If nothing else, would-be assassins made a wonderful distraction.

CHAPTER 13

Lovia ran far and fast from the Den Cade estate. She ran until her lungs burned and her heart pounded so hard, she feared it might burst from her chest. In her mind's eye she still saw Thomison lying in the garden, unmoving. She had neither the strength nor the skill to save him. Her role had been little more than a lookout.

The few potions she'd taken from her grandfather's hidden lab were her sole contribution to the mission and they'd used the ones she considered most valuable. All that remained were two vials of acid and some wound-closing ointment. There were probably other valuable items in the lab, but she didn't know what they were and feared they might blow themselves up if they tried an unfamiliar potion.

Now she wished she'd brought them all and damn the consequences. Lovia would have rather been dead than feel this pain.

When she finally mastered her breathing, she looked around to try and figure out where she'd ended up. Across the street another manor sprawled behind an iron gate. The main house lay so far off the street she couldn't even see it from the road. She looked both ways, but nothing moved.

After an attack on the princess as well as one of the empire's leading families, guards would be everywhere soon enough. Part of Lovia wanted to just stand there and wait. Let the imperial family do with her as they pleased. Without Thomison, what was the point of going on?

She snarled away her self-pity. Were their positions reversed, Thomison would have done everything in his power to avenge her. Lovia would do no less. Unfortunately, the only one she knew that might help her was the overseer and she doubted he would look kindly on her continued failure.

Well, she'd just have to convince him.

But first Lovia had to make it back to their base in First Circle. She dumped her cloak and set out. She'd worn a simple white tunic and brown trousers under her disguise, the sort of outfit no one would look at twice. She doubted anyone had caught a glimpse of her face during the battle. Once she made it out of Third Circle, she should be okay.

She needed only fifteen minutes to reach the wall. Unlike where they entered the circle, this gate had a fully manned guardhouse and a closed portcullis. Lovia wracked her brain. How could she convince them to let her out?

The answer came a moment later. The truth would set her free.

She screamed and broke into a run. "Help! Please, help me!"

A squad of men hurried out to meet her. They looked concerned but not on guard. A single woman didn't look like much of a threat. In fact, she probably looked like a terrified servant.

"What's the trouble, miss?" asked one of the guards, the one in charge she assumed.

"These crazy people attacked Den Cade manor. There are bodies everywhere. Lord Den Cade sent me to get help. You have to do something."

A murmur ran through the guards.

"You'll have to come with us," the guard said.

Lovia's eyes widened. "I'm not going back there. It's a slaughterhouse. All I want is to go home. Please, let me out."

"Come on, sir, we know the way to Den Cade Manor. No need to drag the girl back," one of the other guards said.

Lovia gave a silent thank-you to chivalrous men the world over.

The guard commander made a circle with his finger and the portcullis clanked up. "Go on."

"The One God bless you." Lovia ran out before he changed his mind.

The moment she moved out of sight of the gate she slowed and blew out a breath. Somehow she'd escaped.

The rest of the walk back took nearly an hour. Lucky for her, the gates between First and Second Circle stayed open at all times. Only an invading army or some other emergency would bring them down.

At last she spotted the tenement where the team had met. It seemed a long time ago when all of them were still alive. Now it was just her. The front house and connected warehouse were burned. Literally in the case of the house. Nothing remained save Lovia and their little basement room.

She sighed as she descended the four steps that led to the door. Joining Thomison and the other followers of The One True God had seemed so romantic and exciting when they first met. Lovia had never met anyone like Thomison. He seemed so passionate and determined. Not to mention the magic. Both he and Jenna gained magical abilities through their service to the group. Neither of them, not even after she and Thomison became lovers, had told her how they got their powers. He had simply said once she proved herself, the overseer would reveal more.

Had her grandfather succeeded in assassinating the emperor,

she suspected new powers would have been the reward. Instead, everything fell apart and now she was alone.

Tears started to form and she dashed them away. Her iron key opened the crude lock and she stepped inside. With the door locked behind her, she pulled her final vial out of a hidden pocket and shook it until it glowed blue. Grandfather had given it to her when she was a little girl. Just a toy, but she'd loved it.

By its light she made her way around the table in their combination living room/dining room and went to the back bedroom. No one actually slept here; the room held only a circle of runes that covered the floor. If anyone ever found it, there would be hell to pay. Just to be extra safe, Thomison had paid the building's owner extra to assure their privacy.

The circle connected to wherever the overseer called home. Lovia still hadn't the slightest idea where.

Steeling herself, she stepped into the circle.

Nothing happened. Lovia had never done this by herself. Did Thomison do something to activate the connection? Since none of his powers were visible to her, the possibility certainly existed.

A full minute passed and she had begun to feel foolish standing there when the first mark started to glow with silver light. The rest quickly followed suit and then the pain hit her.

The next thing she knew she stood before the overseer. He sat as usual on his throne under the room's solitary light. He said nothing and even though shadows hid his face, she felt his eyes on her. The feeling, combined with the ever-present stench, left her dizzy.

"You failed again," the overseer said. "I'm impressed you have the courage to stand before me after our last discussion."

"Everyone else is dead. I want peace or revenge. You are the only one I can think of that might give me one or the other."

"I might give you more than that. I might give you an eternity of torment for your endless failures. You've earned nothing better."

"Thomison is dead. My grandfather is dead. What can you do to me that's worse than what has already been done?"

"Oh, you have no idea, little girl. But I am not without sympathy for your situation. I can grant you power. Power enough to lay waste to your enemies. But there is a price. The process is painful and, in the end, you won't really be you anymore."

"What will I be?"

"Both more and less. You will be a vessel for the corruption that dwells in the earth. A force of destruction with little in the way of reason left to you. Eventually that corruption will consume your body, leaving nothing behind."

Lovia shuddered. That sounded beyond horrible. "Is this what The One True God calls for?"

The overseer laughed, a phlegmy, gurgling croak that no human throat had ever made. "Do you know what The One True God is? No, of course you don't. Most of our followers believe we've found some being of power like the false One God. The truth is, The One True God is knowledge. We seek nothing less than the true nature of the universe. We've taken tiny steps toward that end and do you know what we find with every stride?"

She didn't want to know yet found her voice stolen.

"Darkness, evil, and corruption. The greatest power of the universe can be used to dominate, destroy, mutate, and kill. But not create, at least we can't use it that way. Perhaps that will change one day. Now, will you embrace the power or will you let Thomison go unavenged?"

She stiffened at that last sentence. The empire had to pay for taking her love. Even knowing the overseer was using her emotions to manipulate her changed nothing. Whatever it took, Lovia would see the empire pay for its crimes.

"What must I do?"

"Survive."

The overseer leaned forward and she caught a glimpse of a melted face before burning red eyes devoured her and she knew nothing else.

———

"Hello!" someone bellowed from outside the manor. Joran had been about to suggest the little get-together come to an end. His eyelids weighed about five pounds each and if he didn't get to bed soon, he might well fall asleep on the couch.

"What now?" Father stood and stalked toward the door. Joran and the others quickly followed along behind.

They found a detachment of guards standing in the yard, weapons drawn and looking around as if expecting to be attacked at any moment.

"Can I help you?" Father asked.

"Lord Den Cade." His gaze shifted a fraction to look at Alexandra. "And Your Majesty. Forgive the intrusion. We were told many people had been killed."

"By whom?" Alexandra asked.

"The servant Lord Den Cade dispatched. She said assassins attacked the manor."

"We sent no servant," Father said.

"Where is this servant?" Alexandra asked.

"We sent her on her way, Majesty. Poor girl seemed truly shaken."

"Well done, Squad Leader," Alexandra said. "You likely released the only assassin to survive the attack and the only person that could have told us exactly what happened and why."

The man's face had turned the color of a week-dead body. "We didn't know, Majesty."

Alexandra gave a disgusted wave of her hand. If the unfortunate fellow retained his rank, it would be a wonder. So far the guards had let a dozen assassins in and the one survivor out. Not a great showing.

Joran made a mental note to expand his questioning to the city guards. Clearly, they had been infiltrated. Though he suspected this lot were simply in over their heads.

He certainly sympathized.

CHAPTER 14

K night Captain Antius stood in the hold of the Sixth
Legion's dragon ship, toe tapping and arms crossed.
The crewmen watched him with nervous eyes. As if
he might lash out at any moment. He'd have been offended if he
cared what they thought. A White Knight always had himself
fully under control and never killed anyone that didn't deserve
to die.

The ship's captain had made an announcement when Tiber
appeared on the horizon and Antius immediately took up position by the exit ramp. It had taken far too long to arrange for his
return to the capital and he had pressing matters at the church.
Despite repeated requests, he'd only secured his ride because a
messenger bird had arrived summoning the generals back to
Tiber.

No one even complained. Weeks of peace had convinced
everyone that the lizardmen really did want to be good imperial
citizens. Antius had his doubts, but more pressing matters than
the mortal souls of savages required his attention.

He grimaced when he remembered the description the
lizardman had given of the human that warned them of the

empire's pending arrival. Only one White Knight had ever left the order still breathing. Antius remembered the day Bellator had announced he planned a holy quest to retrace the Prophet's journey to Tiber. He'd hoped that by finding that legendary figure's origin, he could gain insight into The One God's wishes for his followers.

Some of the cardinals supported his mission while others said faith alone was enough. In the end, His Holiness the Pope had granted Bellator permission for his quest. The man gathered supplies and set out alone, determined to follow the writings of a monk that claimed to have been with the Prophet at the end of his life.

Antius thought the whole thing mad, but once the pope gave his permission, no one dared question. When years passed and Bellator never returned, they all assumed he'd died on his quest. An honorable way to go, surely, following your faith. He'd believed that was Bellator's fate until that day, surrounded by the dead, on a distant jungle battlefield.

Bellator had returned, now as an enemy of the empire. And the White Knights had to deal with him. He believed wholeheartedly what he'd told Joran Den Cade. This was a church matter and no one else should interfere.

Hopefully His Holiness would agree.

The deck shifted under him and they began the descent to land. At last. With luck he might get to meet with the pope today or tomorrow at the latest.

In truth, that would take nothing short of divine intervention. A cardinal might get in to see the pope on short notice, but not a knight captain.

Fifteen minutes later the dragon ship lurched to a stop. The crewmen tiptoed past him and set to work lowering the boarding ramp. As soon as they got it in place, he strode down into the imperial landing field. Ignoring the palace directly ahead, he turned toward the imposing gray stone church. He'd barely taken a step when the bell rang out four times. Earlier than he'd hoped. Perhaps his meeting had a chance of taking place.

The gate guards gave him no trouble as he left the palace grounds. People seldom gave White Knights trouble, especially when they arrived on dragon ships. The church waited only a hundred yards from the palace grounds. It looked more like a castle than a place of worship. Flying buttresses were decorated with angels in place of gargoyles. Dozens of beautiful stained-glass windows depicting the empire's many victories let light shine into the main chapel.

Antius hurried up the steps leading to a set of glass doors that depicted the Prophet's arrival in Tiber and his meeting with the first Marcus Tiberius. Antius made the circle symbol over his heart and pulled the door open.

Inside he found the huge chapel empty. Hundreds of benches would hold over a thousand worshippers at maximum capacity. The white marble altar at the front of the room had a white cloth covering marked with a crimson circle. Behind that, a sprawling mural depicted all the popes and emperors since the founding.

Antius took a knee and bowed his head, giving thanks to The One God for his safe return. Drawing a circle over his heart once more he stood. One of the doors to the private area of the church behind the altar had opened and a red-robed cardinal stood just inside the chapel. Clean-shaven and gaunt, the cardinal looked like a man shorn of anything save severity and faith. One of the elders, good. Antius found some of the younger cardinals lacked the gravity and focus the position called for.

"Your Grace," Antius said. "I've returned from Stello Province with dire news. Is there any chance I might speak to His Holiness?"

"You are in luck," the cardinal said, his voice raspy and

severe, making it a perfect match for his face. "The pope has been eager for news from the front since Princess Alexandra returned. We had expected a report sooner."

"I returned as soon as possible. Given the distance, I assumed waiting for a departing dragon ship would take less time than going by horse."

"Hmmm. Well, you're here now. Come along and I'll let His Holiness know you've arrived. I'm sure he'll want to speak with you."

Antius's heart leapt and he hurried to follow the cardinal into the back rooms. They walked through plain halls devoid of carpet or tapestries. Only the occasional presence of paintings, all depicting angels, broke the gray monotony. Nothing existed in the church that might distract from contemplating The One God's glory. He approved of this wholeheartedly and wished more of his fellows followed a similar ascetic path. Far too many churchmen indulged in drink and crude behavior.

After a walk long enough to make him think they'd soon reach the back wall, the cardinal stopped in front of a closed door marked with The One God's crimson circle. He knocked twice before opening the door and slipping inside.

Antius's heart sped up. He'd never met the pope. Despite years of service, His Holiness had yet to acknowledge him. This came as no surprise given how much the pope had to do. Keeping the empire on a righteous path no doubt took up most of his time.

After a minute, the door opened again and the cardinal beckoned him in.

The pope's office contrasted starkly with the rest of the church. The whitewashed walls had gold accents and tapestries featuring the crimson circle hung every few feet. The man himself, the mortal representative of The One God, sat behind a golden oak desk. His official vestments hung from a mannequin in the corner. Without the elaborate robes and hat, the pope appeared to be an ordinary middle-aged man.

Antius castigated himself. The clothes didn't make him The One God's chosen servant. Whatever he looked like, this was the most holy leader of the church and he needed to remember that at all times.

He took a knee in front of the desk. "Your Holiness. Thank you for speaking with me."

"Rise, Knight Captain." The pope's voice, like his appearance, seemed an ordinary thing, but Antius felt sure he heard a hint of the divine. "What has happened in Stello Province? Does the war continue?"

"No, Holiness. A peace treaty has been signed between the leaders of the savage tribes and the empire. There have been no attacks since."

"A sudden, if welcome, change of fortune." The pope turned to the cardinal. "Are you ready?"

The crimson-robed man held a board covered in paper as well as a charcoal stick sharpened to a fine point. "Ready, Holiness."

"Then make your report, Knight Captain."

Antius took a deep breath and began. No one else spoke as he detailed everything up until his moment of departure. When he finished, the pope leaned forward, resting his chin on his hands. "Remarkable. What do you make of this serpent?"

Antius shook his head. "I'm uncertain what to make of it. Such a thing should not exist in this world, that is certain. That Bellator knew of it, where to find it, and how to wake it worries me more than the serpent itself. The creature is dead after all, but our former comrade yet lives."

"You're certain the man in white was Bellator?" the cardinal asked.

"I didn't meet him, if that's what you mean. But who else

could he be? All the other White Knights have been accounted for."

"Perhaps Bellator died on his quest and this man calling himself Samaritan found his remains," the pope said. "Or perhaps someone simply made a cloak that resembled a White Knight's. There are many possibilities, yet you jump immediately to the worst of the lot. Why?"

The pope's questioning of his theory made Antius's stomach churn. In truth, he hadn't considered any other theories. When he heard the description, his mind went at once to Bellator and became fixated. Even now, hearing two of many potential alternatives, deep inside Antius believed the former White Knight was Samaritan.

"I don't know, Holiness. I can only say that when I think on it, which I have done a great deal since learning about Samaritan, everything in me says he *is* Bellator. Maybe The One God is sending me a message."

"Maybe," the pope said. "Even if you're wrong, anyone tarnishing the church's name by opposing the empire while dressed as one of our White Knights is clearly an enemy. In any case, he must be dealt with and the sooner the better."

"I volunteer to hunt him down, Holiness," Antius said.

"Have you any idea where to begin your search?" the cardinal asked.

"I... No. My intention was to retrace Bellator's steps in the hope that I'd find a clue."

"A dim prospect I fear," the pope said.

Once again having his thoughts questioned by the pope left a sick feeling in Antius's stomach. He had spent many hours fantasizing about this meeting and in his dreams, it never went this way.

"Fortunately, I have a solution for your problem." The pope ran a hand over his face. He looked tired. No doubt the weight of his many responsibilities exhausted him. "Though it is not well known, when Bellator didn't return after a full year, I ordered a search party dispatched to find him."

Antius's eyes went wide. He'd heard nothing about that.

"They returned after six months, having seen no sign of him. We all assumed he'd died on the journey. If we were wrong, you might pick up where they left off."

"Are the members of the rescue party church members?" Antius asked.

"They aren't White Knights, if that's what you mean," the pope said. "But they are devout members of the congregation. A team of specialists we've used on those occasions when our missionaries came under attack in distant provinces. They are highly skilled and experienced both in combat and exploration. I will summon them and when they arrive you will set out together. Whoever this Samaritan is, I want you to bring back his head along with Bellator's white cloak. The cloak will be honored and the head burned."

Antius made the circle over his heart. He would have preferred to take fellow White Knights on the hunt, but if these specialists could shorten the search, he would be a fool to refuse. Not that he had the authority to refuse a command from the pope in any case.

"I will rest and pray while I await your orders."

"That is well," the pope said. "Go now."

Antius withdrew and made his way toward the chapel. He had no need of the cardinal to guide him down the straight path. With the start of his mission in sight, Antius should have felt nothing but joy. Instead, he had to fight the feeling that some lurking darkness hid just out of sight, waiting to devour him.

———

Septimus Salonius, or as most people called him, His Holiness the Pope, rubbed his face and sighed. No wonder everyone hated White Knights. Dealing with someone like…

"What was that idiot's name, anyway?" he asked.

Cardinal Rufious cocked his head in thought. "Antius, I believe. One of our most devoted holy warriors."

"Doubtless. What do you make of his story?"

"I'm certain he told the truth. It would never occur to him to lie, especially not to you. As for what it all means, the answer to that question will take longer to ascertain. I share his concern for the fallen White Knight, especially since he's supposed to be dead. I also think Antius is far too quick to dismiss the serpent just because it is dead. There may be more of them out there and if so, who knows what mischief the empire's enemies might get up to."

"The emperor no doubt shares your concern. Summon the hunters. They failed to kill him the last time they went out; time to clean up their mistake."

"I'll reread their report as well," Rufious said. "Clearly they either lied or left something out. Do you suppose it would be better to find new hunters?"

Septimus pushed away from the desk, stood, and stretched. The tension of his meeting left his body aching. He wanted to spend an hour with the nuns, not worry about overzealous White Knights. They were supposed to die fighting the empire's enemies, not live to cause trouble for their betters.

"Where are the hunters anyway?" Septimus asked.

"No doubt drinking and whoring in Drobeta. I'll send a messenger at once to fetch them." Rufious's severe expression softened. "You look all in. Why don't you take a rest?"

"What about that thing the emperor wanted me to attend this evening?"

"You're the pope. Who's going to complain? If anyone says anything we'll tell them you were lost in prayer or something."

Septimus grinned. "That does sound appropriately holy, doesn't it? Very well, you've convinced me. Oh, and have someone keep an eye on Antius. He strikes me as the determined sort."

"I got that impression as well. I'll take care of him."

"Many thanks, Rufious. If you need me, I'll be with the nuns."

CHAPTER 15

Joran licked his dry lips and tried to relax. He stood beside Alexandra in a little niche to the right of the throne room out of sight of the many nobles and generals assembled to hear the emperor's announcement. Despite having a week to make peace with his new situation, Joran still had trouble wrapping his mind around the idea that he and Alexandra were to marry. He dearly would have liked Mia at his side, but she'd ended up among the guards lining the throne room.

At least after the attack at the manor, Joran's parents hadn't uttered a word of complaint when he mentioned adopting her. The process had begun, but as with all things bureaucratic, it would take time to finish. Given everything that had happened, Joran hoped they were still alive to celebrate.

"You're fidgeting," Alexandra said. "Stop it."

Joran only noticed his finger tapping against his thigh when she mentioned it. "Sorry, I'm a bit nervous. It's not every day the emperor announces you're joining the imperial family. I think I'd rather fight another giant serpent."

"Oh, it's not that bad. Father will make a little speech about why you're qualified to marry me, we'll go out, everyone will clap as they pretend to be happy for us, then we'll have to mingle for an hour or two. No monsters, no assassins, just liars and backstabbers."

"Swell. Just to make this dog-and-pony show worthwhile I drank a detect-deception potion. It'll probably make my head explode, but I'm curious to see if any of the nobles have heard of The One True God cult. The trick will be bringing it up in such a way that I don't arouse suspicion."

Alexandra shook her head. "I wouldn't risk it, not here anyway. Anything that hints at weakness will be a problem for us, especially after Father's recent sickness. Marcus says the nobles were circling like vultures when he hadn't put in an appearance for a few weeks. I don't know what they think they'll accomplish if our family falls. Any amount of internal squabbling will see the empire torn apart, either from within or from one of our neighbors invading a province. Stupid, short-sighted idiots."

"That about perfectly describes most of the nobles. If it's your preference, I'll be sure to keep to small talk."

Trumpets blared a fanfare and a loud voice announced, "His Imperial Majesty, Marcus Tiberius the Twenty-Sixth!"

A door creaked open and a cheer filled the air.

"At least they're good at pretending to care," Joran said.

"The nobles have to be good at something."

After a few minutes, the cheers died down to nothing and the emperor said, "Thank you, ladies and gentlemen, for the warm welcome. It's been too long since I had a chance to see you all."

"Your father does a fair impression of liking them as well."

"Oh, yes. Father lies to them and they lie to him all the while they try and figure out how to undermine each other or in Father's case hope to find something illegal so he can blackmail the worst offenders. It's a hideous drain on imperial resources.

The rest of the world should be grateful we spend as much time arguing amongst ourselves as we do. If we actually focused, we might have conquered the continent by now."

"I have some important announcements," the emperor continued. "First, thanks to the outstanding work of our legions in Stello Province, we have brought that campaign to a successful conclusion. A peace treaty has been signed with the local populace that will allow trade to flourish."

This brought a fresh round of applause. Much like Joran's family, most of the nobles invested in various merchant interests. The prospect of new markets as well as new imports no doubt had them drooling.

"Next and most exciting for me, I have selected a husband for my daughter. Most of you are no doubt familiar with the Den Cade family. The youngest son has done many great services for the empire, including negotiating the peace treaty in Stello Province and saving Alexandra's life several times."

The emperor went on, praising Joran in lavish style. Joran turned to Alexandra. "Are we not supposed to mention the serpent or your father's recent illness as well as Cordius's betrayal?"

"The serpent is fine. Too many soldiers saw it to pretend it didn't exist. Father's illness should never be mentioned as life-threatening and Cordius has retired to spend more time with his family. In another couple weeks we'll make it known that he died of natural causes and we'll have a funeral befitting a man that served the imperial family for decades."

"You didn't think to mention any of these lies before now?"

"Things have been hectic."

"Please welcome my daughter and future son-in-law," the emperor said at last.

Joran took Alexandra's hand and they walked out side by side. The gathered rich and powerful cheered as they were expected to, polite devils. He looked out over the sixty or so nobles as well as generals both familiar and new. Only General Ventor, Alexandra's second-in-command, refused to clap. He stood, arms crossed, looking furious about the whole situation. No doubt he thought one day he'd be standing where Joran was. A part of Joran would have happily traded places with him. But another part, perhaps an arrogant part, believed he needed to be here if he wanted to save the empire from the forces that wanted to destroy it.

The emperor stood up from his golden throne and hugged Alexandra and then Joran. He looked perfectly strong and healthy; head up, shoulders back and dressed in his fur-trimmed purple robes of state. If Joran hadn't known he'd nearly died not that long ago, he wouldn't have believed it.

The three of them turned to face the audience and Alexandra and her father waved. Joran belatedly joined in. He vaguely remembered Father taking him and his brothers to a First Circle sideshow when they were little. The main attraction was a two-headed goat. Joran finally understood how that goat must have felt having all those people staring at it. When this— whatever it was—ended, he hoped someone gave him something better than hay to eat.

They stopped waving after about thirty seconds and Joran whispered, "What now?"

"Now you mingle," Alexandra said. "Smile a lot and promise nothing. Everyone here wants something from you. You can't give them anything, but they don't realize that yet. Once they do, you'll be fine."

The trio split up and Joran went left. He'd never visited the throne room before. His entire apartment building could have fit in the room with plenty of space to spare. Ten white marble pillars as big as tree trunks supported the vaulted ceiling and tables covered with food and wine glasses ran up and down both sides.

Joran made it fifteen feet from the throne before the first

noble latched on to him. The fat man grabbed Joran's arm and guided him away from a little knot of his compatriots. He dressed in crimson silk highlighted by gold rings and a diamond pendant.

"Congratulations on your engagement. I've heard tales of your harrowing battle with the serpent monster. It must have been terrifying."

"I had help, but yes, fighting a fifty-yard-long serpent certainly qualifies as terrifying."

"You're an alchemist too I understand. A grandmaster no less. Remarkable. When can we expect a new little addition to the imperial family?"

"Alexandra and I aren't even married yet."

The nobleman blanched slightly. "Of course. I didn't mean to imply that you two would do anything inappropriate. Though she is a beautiful woman."

He winked at Joran who kept his expression neutral. "You're right about that. I should probably chat with some of the others. Unless there's something else you wish to discuss?"

If the nobleman wanted to offer a bribe, make a threat, or ask for a favor, hopefully Joran's prompt would get him to the point.

"No, no, I just wanted to offer my well wishes." The nobleman released him and waddled off to the food table.

Joran went the opposite way and nearly ran straight into General Ventor. His broad shoulders strained the crimson robe he wore and his chiseled face twisted in an ugly frown.

"Afternoon, General," Joran said. "All's well in Cularo, I trust?"

"It should be me marrying the princess, not a useless weakling like you. How can you protect her? She needs a strong man to stand beside her. The empire needs that as well."

Joran glanced to his right. "The emperor is over there and unoccupied at the moment. If you'd like to point out all the reasons he should change his mind about Alexandra's future husband, I'm sure he'd be delighted to listen to your thoughts."

Ventor's jaw bunched and Joran imagined he heard the man's teeth grinding. "Perhaps another time. One thing is certain—you won't last a year as her husband. When you die, she'll need a shoulder to cry on. That will be my chance."

"I'm not sure what I find more amusing, that you imagine your threat a subtle one or that you think if you succeed in killing me, the Iron Princess will cry on your shoulder. You have met Alexandra, right?"

Ventor snarled something unintelligible before stalking off.

Now not only did he have a cult that wanted him dead, but a general as well. He shuddered to think how many other enemies he might pick up before the end of this little get-together.

CHAPTER 16

Alexandra had years of experience dealing with nobles and their scheming. Deflecting their questions about Joran and his family came as natural as breathing. Every time she glanced Joran's way, he appeared to be holding his own. Only when he had a tense conversation with Ventor did Alexandra feel a moment of anxiety.

No servants mingled with the great and powerful today. The nobles were forced to collect their own snacks and drinks from the tables running along both sides of the throne room. Father hadn't wanted any more eyes than necessary to see any mistakes the newest member of the imperial family might make. But even Father would have to admit Joran had done well.

At least the public proclamation wouldn't require another of these get-togethers. The imperial messengers would spread word through the city before expanding out to the rest of the home district and then the provinces.

Even more impressive than Joran's performance was her father's. He seemed as strong as ever and he dealt firmly with everyone he spoke to. Nothing like a properly prepared cure all to set a person right. And she should know.

She spotted Joran standing alone for a moment and went to check on him. "Still alive, I see."

He offered a weak smile. "Barely. Ventor made clear that, should the opportunity arise, he'd be happy to sort that out for me. That way you'd turn to him for comfort."

Alexandra snorted. "In his dreams maybe. Perhaps Ventor is in need of a new post. Somewhere far away from us."

"If you're serious, that might present us with an opportunity. Send him to some backwater fort and assign a spy to watch him. A disgruntled general would make a tempting potential recruit for our enemies. Depending on his actions, we might be able to deal with Ventor and whoever contacts him."

Alexandra took his hand and smiled. "You're going to fit right in with my family."

"I'm uncertain if that's a compliment. Speaking of your family... Where's your brother?"

"Marcus begged off. He's spent so much time at Father's side, he wanted an afternoon with his wife and kids."

Trumpets blew and the throne room doors opened.

"Ladies and gentlemen," Father said. "We thank you for joining us on this joyous occasion. Have a safe journey home."

The nobles needed no further prompting and began streaming out of the throne room. Father caught her eye and waved her over.

"I'll head back to your suite," Joran said.

"You're not escaping that easily." Alexandra dragged him along to join her father near the throne.

Father grinned at Joran as they approached. "You did well, my boy. If I didn't know better, I'd have thought you'd been doing this all your life."

"I might not get a lot of practice, thank The One God, but Mother made sure I had thorough training when it comes to dealing with the nobility."

"What about your father?" he asked.

"Father was all about business and adventure. He taught me to ride horses, survive in the wild, that sort of thing. He even tried to teach me the sword, but I had no aptitude."

"A broad education then, good. That will serve you well." Alexandra tensed slightly when Father turned to look at her. "I thought we might have dinner with Marcus tonight. Just the family."

She glanced at Joran but Father immediately added, "The immediate family."

"No problem," Joran said. "Mia and I can get something from the kitchen. I'd been hoping to do some reading anyway. See you both later."

He bowed and hurried away, Mia falling in beside him as they reached the door.

"A remarkable young man," Father said when they'd gone. "You did well recruiting him. Joran Den Cade may well be just the man we need to smoke out the empire's enemies. And should he fail, we'll have lost only the youngest son of a minor noble family, freeing you to marry someone higher ranking."

Alexandra stared, aghast but hardly surprised. "What about finding someone that will make me happy? You sounded like that was a priority."

"Don't be such a child. Your happiness is a good deal less important than the well-being of the empire. I'll promise you to as many people as it takes to ensure the empire's longevity. Let's go eat, I'm sure your brother is growing impatient."

Alexandra followed him out of the throne room numb inside and cold as a statue. She'd always known that her father would use anyone and anything, but hearing him say it out loud and in such a bold-faced way left her empty.

Alexandra glanced over her shoulder at the door where Joran had left. He'd shown her more kindness than her own blood relatives. Maybe she needed to rethink where her true loyalties lay.

———

That night Joran rested on the couch in Alexandra's suite. Maybe he should try and think of it as their suite. No, everything in the palace was hers. Only a fool would try and convince himself otherwise. He glanced at Mia who had fallen sound asleep in one of the chairs. He feared his stress had worn her out more than him; he'd managed to escape the noble chattering with only a mild headache.

Alexandra had needed to speak with her father and brother about family matters or something that didn't concern him. Since he had no interest in further talking, Joran hadn't pointed out that he would be family in half a year.

Instead, he'd happily retreated to the peace and quiet of the suite, eaten a simple dinner, and settled in to read. He'd been looking for a quiet moment to take a look at the journal he'd found in Samaritan's lab, but simply hadn't had the time. Well, he had the time now.

He flipped open the first page and nodded to himself. Excellent penmanship, just as they taught at the imperial college. He'd had no doubts about Samaritan's lineage, but everything he'd seen just drove it home all the harder. The man that tried to destroy the empire was without a doubt an imperial and possibly a noble. Hopefully the journal would shed some light on why someone with excellent prospects would want to ruin the one place he could best take advantage of them.

The book started with his arrival in Stello Province. Too bad, Joran would have liked to know more about his earlier journey and how he ended up in the jungle.

After Samaritan arrived, he'd spent some time exploring the jungle, searching for the mountain where he hoped to find a weapon he'd learned about in his research. Where he'd done this research also wasn't mentioned. Pity.

It went on to describe his thoughts about the natives in

rather ugly terms. Generally regarding them as primitive savages whose take on magic displayed their ignorance for all to see. Yet more proof of his noble lineage. The only interesting note focused on their spirit worship. According to Samaritan, what the native shamans perceived as spirits was, in fact, an energy field called the ether. Joran had never heard that phrase before.

He scanned through, searching for more references. He found it about halfway through. After they located the serpent's hiding place, Samaritan described the monster's presence and how it twisted and corrupted the ether. Since the ether and spirits were the same, that pretty much confirmed Joran's theory that the serpent had somehow enchanted the natives' Holy Ones.

The next reference mentioned how the corrupted ether affected his alchemy. Joran frowned. He never really thought of alchemy working through the same medium as the magic of the people they conquered. He'd always considered it more elevated. Special. But if in the end alchemy represented nothing more than another branch of the same magical river, what did that mean for the empire and the church? The primacy of alchemy as taught to them by the Prophet served as one of the central premises of the empire's founding.

If that turned out to be a lie, what else might?

Joran put the journal back in his pack. For now, at least, he dared tell no one except Mia what he'd learned. Trying to keep a secret from her would only give him a worse headache.

The door burst open and a furious Alexandra marched in. She looked like she wanted to kill someone. Joran didn't think he had done or said anything to upset her, so hopefully some other poor devil had drawn her wrath.

"The family meeting not go well?" Joran asked.

"No, it didn't. Come with me." Her tone made it clear an argument would not be welcome.

He rolled to his feet and followed her into her bedroom. It wasn't all that much bigger than the guest room he shared with Mia. Only the bed looked different, a little wider with a white silk canopy.

"So what happened?" he asked.

"Father made it clear that, despite his lofty talk about making me happy and rewarding you for all you'd done for the empire, he really just wants to use you to clean up his many problems and should you die in the process, no great loss."

"Oh, is that all?"

"Is that all!?" She rounded on him. "Aren't you mad?"

"Not especially. I mean, I didn't exactly take the emperor at his word. No one in his position can let something as simple as feelings decide stuff like this. The idea that I was stupid enough to buy his line of nonsense offended me more than anything. I guess he felt like he couldn't come straight out and say he wanted to use us—that's Mia and me, you too I suppose. If it makes you feel better, I don't mind playing along since I want access to resources I can't get on my own. We can use each other, like proper imperial nobles."

"You're as bad as Father!" She reached behind her, trying to undo the buttons holding her dress on. Clearly the designer intended for servants to lend a hand as she didn't even come close to reaching them.

"Let me." Joran turned her around and gently undid the buttons. "There."

She let the dress fall to the floor, revealing the thin silk shift underneath. "Thank you. I swear I thought that thing was going to suffocate me. I'm sorry about Father, even if you don't seem upset. I guess I gave him too much credit."

Alexandra leaned back against him and Joran debated where to put his hands. He settled on her shoulders and tried to rub some of the tension out of them. Her groan of pleasure indicated success.

"Just out of curiosity, assuming I actually live until spring, does he plan to let the wedding go on, or will I end up having to spend more time with my family before dying of natural causes?"

"Since he announced it to the gathered nobility, he'll have to go through with it. And frankly, given everything that's happening, you'll have earned it and then some."

Joran worked his hands a little further down her chest.

She immediately pulled away and spun to face him.

He raised his hands. "Sorry. Too soon?"

"No. I mean, yes. I mean, I don't know. It's just...I've never, you know."

Joran stared at her and thought back on the various flirting, teasing, and inuendo. "Seriously? I got the impression you were fairly, um, experienced."

Alexandra sat on the edge of her bed and hung her head. "It's all an act. The whole Iron Princess persona. Being the supreme commander of the army comes with certain expectations. One of them is that you're a hard-drinking, tough-as-nails warrior, who's as willing to kill an enemy as jump into bed with any guy lucky enough to catch your eye. I have little more experience personally killing people than I do sleeping with them."

She looked up. Tears had mixed with her makeup to create blue streaks that ran down her cheeks. "Why would anyone follow a virgin that's never killed anyone with her own hands? The men respect me because they think I'm their Iron Princess. If the truth ever came out..."

Joran sat beside her and put his arm around her shoulders. She'd told him nothing but the truth—the potion he'd drunk earlier confirmed that. Lucky for him the effect lingered as he might have feared she wanted to manipulate him with her story.

"Let's make a deal," he said. "I'll help you be the best Iron Princess you can be and when it's just the two of us, you can be Alexandra. No pressure, no acting, just be yourself."

She shifted enough to look into his eyes. "What's in it for you?"

Ah, the eternal question that must be asked of any noble. "I have one small hope. Having seen the real you, even if only a tiny piece, I hope that in time, as we get to know each other—the real us, not the faces we show the world—we might find love. A stupid, romantic notion, I know. But the truth all the same. In six months, I would very much like to still be alive and have the chance to marry someone I can really love. Sound appealing?"

Alexandra wrapped her arms around him. "Very."

She washed her face and snuggled under the covers. Joran stayed with her until she fell asleep. Her face, relaxed and at ease, brought a smile to his lips. She'd done a fine job convincing him that the Iron Princess was reality. Now that he'd seen the truth, a warm, protective feeling had settled over Joran. He'd find some way to get them through this and come spring, he would hopefully marry the real Alexandra.

Leaving her to sleep, Joran slipped out into the living room.

Mia sat up in her chair, wide awake. "That felt way less intense than I'd expected. Shouldn't you two be cuddling and enjoying the afterglow?"

Joran shook his head and nodded toward the room they shared. He collected his kit on the way. He didn't need the servants stumbling onto Samaritan's journal. When the bedroom door shut, Joran told Mia everything from both the journal and Alexandra.

"She was such a mess. I felt like I'd have been taking advantage, especially if it's her first time."

Mia gaped at him. "Wow. I had no idea. None of the Iron Guards did. She always seemed so confident and sexy. It's really all an act?"

"Afraid so. I'll be counting on you to help me with her. Mostly I'll need you to not act like anything's changed. People will expect a new couple to act different around each other, but if others notice that the Iron Princess isn't as tough as they thought, that might cause trouble."

"No kidding. The generals would jump at any excuse to get out from under her thumb. Of course, even if she wasn't the Iron Princess, she would still be the emperor's daughter and a brilliant commander."

Joran yawned. "Hopefully it doesn't come to her simply resorting to threatening to tell Daddy if they disobey. I'm all in. Let's call it a night."

"Right. We want to be well rested for whatever problems arise tomorrow."

Joran chuckled. "That's the spirit."

They changed into their night clothes and Joran fell asleep wondering how much more complicated his life could get.

CHAPTER 17

Pope Septimus Salonius sat behind the desk in his office. He wore his gaudy, uncomfortable formal robes and the three-foot-tall hat. Rufious stood at his right hand in his crimson cardinal's robes. Septimus has tested the fabric and found it much softer than his white and gold outfit. That seemed wrong since he was the pope. When he pointed it out, Rufious had said the people appreciated that their divine guide didn't wallow in comforts they would never know.

That struck Septimus as stupid since he frequently wallowed to his heart's content and besides, no one would ever find out how coarse his robes were.

"So where are these hunters anyway? Don't they know it's rude to keep the most powerful man in the empire waiting?"

"They arrived in Tiber this morning and were told to come directly to the church. I assume they'll be here momentarily."

Septimus muttered something unkind, though whether he directed his venom at the late hunters or his cardinal, he hadn't made up his mind. It was the scratchy robes talking anyway. He had nothing pressing on his schedule today.

Five minutes later a knock sounded on his office door and

one of the lesser priests stuck his head in. "Your guests are here, Holiness."

"Show them in, please," Septimus said, doing his best to sound magnanimous. Sometimes playing the role of the kind-hearted holy man took a lot of effort. Though it always seemed to please his underlings.

A few seconds later four rough-looking men and an equally battered woman strode into his office. They wore a mix of leather and chain armor and each of them carried a small arsenal. Under different circumstances, they never would have been allowed in his presence armed as they were, but these five had served the church well for many years and in so doing earned a measure of his trust. Of course, it didn't hurt that there was a button under his desk he could push to flood the room with a particularly lethal poison to which he and Rufious were immune.

"Holiness," said Trupo, a nondescript imperial commoner and the group's leader. "How may we be of service?"

"Do you remember some years ago," Septimus asked, "when I sent you on a mission to eliminate a wayward White Knight who sought answers to questions better left unasked?"

"I do, Holiness. That was our first mission beyond the empire's borders," Trupo said.

"I'm pleased to hear that. In your report, you claimed that you successfully dealt with the White Knight we sent you to kill. Could you elaborate on exactly how you completed your mission?" Septimus asked.

"We tracked him northeast, through rough country. It took several months before we finally caught up with him. When we did, we found that he had acquired a companion along his journey. During the initial battle we killed the companion, but the White Knight escaped. I don't know what drove him, but it took us two days to finally catch up. When we did, we found him standing at the edge of a high cliff. When he saw us coming he leapt. The fall had to be at least three hundred feet. No one could've survived."

"You saw the body?" Septimus asked.

"We didn't climb down, if that's what you mean. From that height there wouldn't have been enough left of him to bury. What is this about, Holiness?"

"It seems the White Knight you were supposed to have killed has returned and bears the empire a considerable grudge. He's already cost us a great deal of lives and gold. It's time for you to fix your mistake."

Trupo shook his head, his disbelief clear. "No mortal man could've survived that fall. Perhaps someone else found his gear and claimed it."

"I see." Septimus steepled his fingers. "Your theory is that some other noble from the empire found that spot so far to the northeast, climbed down the cliff, and claimed the cloak and armor of the dead White Knight. How likely does that seem to you?"

"Not very," Trupo admitted. "But having seen the cliff, I consider it more likely than anyone falling from that height surviving. But regardless, if you wish us to hunt down this man causing you trouble, we will, of course, do our best to send him to meet The One God as quickly as possible. Simply point us in the proper direction."

"I appreciate your attitude, Trupo," Septimus said. "Rufious, fill them in."

The cardinal cleared his throat. "The man in question was last seen in Stello Province using the name Samaritan. He worked to rile up the natives, causing unnecessary death and destruction before fleeing to avoid the empire's wrath. We have little confidence that he remains in the area and the local lizardmen are unlikely to have more information. Given the circumstances, your best bet is to return to where you last saw Samaritan and begin searching for anything nearby. The man clearly gained access to some forbidden knowledge. Our guess is in some ruins or something in the area."

"That's a lot of guesses and maybes, Cardinal," Trupo said. "Do you have anything solid?"

"Unfortunately, no. We also have another White Knight determined to bring his fallen brother to justice. We can't have him hanging around here, so he'll be joining you. Should it be necessary, he is decidedly expendable."

"Only this time, if you have to kill him, make sure he's actually dead," Septimus said. "We need no more loose ends."

Trupo winced and nodded. "Count on us, Holiness. Where can we find our new companion? We'll leave at once."

"His name is Antius and you should find him in the barracks or thereabouts," Rufious said. "He's expecting you, though he thinks you're trackers who are coming to guide him on his holy quest or something equally stupid. Play along as best you can."

The five hunters bowed and withdrew.

When they'd gone Septimus tossed his hat aside and blew out a long breath. "They'd better not screw up this time."

Rufious made the circle over his heart. "We can only pray."

Antius stood up from his spot in front of the barracks' small altar and made a circle over his heart. He completed his prayer, the same prayer he'd offered three times a day since His Holiness said trackers would arrive soon to help him locate Bellator. So far, The One God hadn't seen fit to answer his prayer. Instead, it seemed his patience was to be tested. Antius knew how to wait and would do so for as long as necessary. His only worry was that every moment Bellator got farther and farther away. The renegade had to be brought to justice and Antius had to be the one that did it.

No one else would truly understand, but Antius had admired

Bellator before he went on his quest. That admiration in the face of what turned out to be a huge betrayal meant that his instincts weren't as keen as he'd believed. If they led him wrong here, where else might they take him down the wrong path? He had to figure out what happened or he would never trust himself again. And a White Knight whose faith had been shaken served no good purpose.

The barracks door opened and he didn't even have to turn around. "You have come to guide me in the hunt for the traitor."

"If your name is Antius then yes, we have come to guide you at His Holiness's command. My name is Trupo and I lead this band of hunters. We are ready to depart as soon as you are."

Antius finally turned and found himself face-to-face with the roughest crew of mercenaries he had ever seen. It strained the imagination to believe they were servants of the holy church, yet their leader spoke with great respect when he mentioned the pope. The One God worked in mysterious ways and if these were his chosen agents, then so be it.

"I am prepared to leave at this moment, assuming you have the supplies we'll need assembled."

"We have, sir," Trupo said. "When His Holiness summons us, we know a great journey awaits."

Antius nodded. The more he heard this fellow speak, the more confident he felt that he'd found a kindred spirit. His appearance aside, Trupo clearly had a strong faith. In the end, that mattered far more than the clothes a man wore.

Antius collected his sword from the bench it leaned against. "Then lead on."

Outside the barracks waited six saddled horses and three heavily laden mules. Antius gaped. Just how far were they going to have to go?

The trackers said nothing as they swung up onto their mounts, leaving a single horse waiting for him. "Where is this journey to take us?"

"Northeast," Trupo said. None of his subordinates had made a sound so far. Their discipline further heartened Antius. "Beyond the empire. Cardinal Rufious suggested we retrace Samaritan's, or Bellator's as you prefer, steps in the hopes of finding his lair. The assumption is that he's no longer in Stello Province and that attempting to investigate on that end would be a waste of time. You're the only person I've spoken to that has actually been to Stello Province. Do you agree with the cardinal's assessment?"

Antius considered the question and immediately nodded. The cardinal's reasoning made sense and given his own doubts about his instincts, Antius wouldn't have questioned even had he disagreed.

He swung up onto the final horse. "Yes, I agree. The natives are unlikely to know anything about Bellator's true plans."

"Excellent. I have great faith in the cardinal's reasoning, but it's always good to hear from somebody with firsthand knowledge of the situation."

They rode through the city and out the north gate. Antius knew little about what lay to the northeast. The empire had expanded north and west as far as the dwarves' homeland. And due west to within a score or so miles of the Land of the Blood Drinkers. But northeast remained a mystery. What little he knew came from reading atlases and they said only that great forests of towering trees filled the area. Certainly they detailed nothing that should have drawn the attention of a man questing for the Prophet's origin.

Perhaps Bellator had learned something from the Prophet's final interview. Antius had tried to find the book himself, but it no longer resided in the imperial library. He suspected the Inquisition had claimed it fearing someone else following in Bellator's footsteps.

Considering how that first quest had turned out, that might

have been a wise decision. Though what it meant for his own mission, Antius hesitated to contemplate.

———

S amaritan woke from a long sleep. He always needed a huge amount of rest after a major use of magic. He felt so weak, but forced himself to roll out of bed and find food and drink. Not that he had a huge selection. In a sealed trunk he kept dried meat and vegetables along with several jars of water. A circle of stones in the corner of his temporary home served as a stove. He tossed a few chunks of wood into the circle and pointed. The ether crackled and the wood burst into flame. A simple soup soon simmered over the fire.

While it cooked, he shuffled over to the workbench opposite his bed. The few alchemy supplies he had left wouldn't make more than a handful of simple potions. He needed to restock, but finding what he needed out here would be next to impossible. Instead, he focused on the book at the end of the table, the greatest treasure he'd ever found.

Not that most others would consider it a great treasure. It didn't hold potion recipes or spells. In fact, it was a history book, an ancient one, detailing some experiments conducted by an empire that existed thousands of years ago. Much as Samaritan despised the Tiberian Empire, their petty evils didn't hold a candle to this one. These wizards corrupted the flesh of men and beasts to create monsters that they used to destroy their enemies.

The most powerful of those monsters were giant beasts so strong even the wizards that made them failed to fully control their power. Recognizing the danger, they'd hidden them away, cursed to sleep in the earth for all eternity.

The empire would have stood all of time, but for the arrogance of its rulers. Like all powerful men—Samaritan thought of them as men even though he had serious doubts about their actual humanity—they constantly sought more power. Eventually they found the greatest power in the world and it destroyed them and everything around them. The ruin Samaritan called home had been one of their most far-flung outposts and even it took major damage.

That was the power he sought. The power to wipe the Tiberian Empire from the map and reset the world to a primal state. Perhaps humanity could do a better job when they rebuilt this time. His smile held nothing but bitterness. More likely another empire would rise, crushing the weak, and expanding ever outward until someone like him showed up and brought it to its knees.

Of course, that assumed that he actually found the now-sleeping power. The history book held a great deal of information about their experiments, but said nothing about the great beast's resting place.

So he contented himself with finding the lesser monsters and doing as much damage as possible while he searched for more clues.

His soup bubbled and he took it off the fire. Before he had a chance to taste it, his silver amulet grew warm.

Setting the pot down to cool he touched the smooth metal and focused his will. "Go ahead."

"The serpent proved as impressive as you said it would." The Archbishop—Samaritan knew the woman by no other name—said in her cool, controlled tone. "Pity the enemy killed it before it did any real damage."

"True enough. If only I had some way to control the beasts. But if the ancient wizards failed, my meager power certainly isn't enough. Did you want something?"

"Only to share a warning. One of our agents spotted a group leaving the empire and heading northeast. The only reason I can imagine for them to do that is to hunt you. A White Knight led them."

Samaritan grimaced. A White Knight. One of his former comrades would never give up until he found Samaritan and brought him to justice for his supposed crimes. Once word got out that someone dressed as one of their precious order had attacked the empire, it was only a matter of time before they had to act. He would take great pleasure in killing whoever they sent.

"Thank you for the warning, Archbishop."

"What are allies for?" Her voice held a mocking lilt. "When will you go to search for the next beast?"

"As soon as I've dealt with the church's hunters. Will your people meet me at the pass?"

"It will be as we discussed. Contact me when you arrive and I will alert them."

"Understood. Is there anything else?"

"No." The archbishop's presence vanished and he released the amulet.

Samaritan smiled at the prospect of killing some of the church's dogs. He ate with a will, hate fueling his hunger. If they were heading northeast, he knew where they had to be going. And he knew the perfect way to kill them.

CHAPTER 18

Lovia floated, surrounded by darkness and pain. Her screams had ended she knew not how long ago. Now she seemed to experience the pain from a distance, as if aware it existed, but in an abstract way, like the one feeling the pain wasn't really her.

She tried to move, to look another way, to see something in the endless darkness. Perhaps she succeeded and there was simply nothing to see. Or maybe she failed and some force bound her in place. She had no idea either way. No idea what the overseer did to her.

That he had done something horrible she had no doubt. That last image of his melted face, the skin dripping like candle wax, and those burning, demonic eyes, would haunt her for however long her life lasted. Assuming she hadn't already died and ended up in hell.

A tiny red dot appeared before her. She tried to reach for it, but again found herself unable to move.

The dot moved closer and a garbled sound reached her. Light and sound, that meant she still lived, didn't it? She thought it did.

"Wake up, Lovia."

That voice. She knew it well. The overseer spoke to her.

"It's time to come back and avenge Thomison."

At the mention of her lover, her anger roared to life. Lethargy burned away and with it the darkness. She stared up into the overseer's burning eyes. His face looked no better than before and he'd shed the cloak that usually obscured his features. She'd once thought he wore that cloak to hide his identity, but now she understood the truth. He wore it so his subordinates wouldn't see his true nature. That he'd allowed Lovia to see his true appearance seemed a bad omen.

"What happened? What did you do to me?" she asked.

"I granted your wish. I gave you the power to destroy those that took the one you loved. Your will to survive impressed me. Many others have gone through the conversion process, but you are the first—" his face twisted into a freakish parody of a smile "—well, second, to survive the ritual with your mind and sense of self intact. Stand and see what you've become."

Lovia felt around and found flat stone under her fingers. She seemed to be lying on a stone table of some sort. Her sense of touch seemed muted. The hard, rough surface barely registered. Sight and hearing seemed unaffected though she smelled nothing and tasted only a bitter, acidic bile.

Finally, she pushed away and staggered to her feet. She almost fell. The lack of touch made her unsteady. A few steps later she started to get the hang of it.

The stone chamber she woke in looked different than the one with the overseer's throne. This one held four more stone tables like the one she'd been lying on. Three people? No, calling the figures people did actual people no justice. They looked like corpses with black ooze dripping from empty eye sockets. She'd never seen anything like them and hoped to never do so again.

"Rather unattractive, aren't they?" the overseer asked. "Not that I'm one to talk. I've done better work, I admit, but they have their uses all the same. For now let's focus on you. You've noticed, I assume, that your body no longer registers pain like before."

"Yes. It's like I'm aware something has happened to me, but it doesn't impair my movement or thinking."

"Precisely correct. You've become something more than human, something greater. I could run a sword through your chest and you'd barely note it. The wound would heal in moments. You are essentially unkillable."

"What happens now?" she asked.

"Now I send you back to Tiber where you go on a rampage. Slaughter your way through the city until you find those responsible for Thomison's death. Do as much damage as you can. Subtle means have failed to accomplish our goals, perhaps brute force will be more successful." The overseer took a step before turning back. "I recommend against trying anything sneaky. Much like myself, you no longer blend in with ordinary people."

Lovia had an overwhelming desire for a mirror, but the chamber held nothing reflective. From what she'd seen, no one here would have any desire to see themselves. That boded ill for her.

They left the stone-table room and entered the room where they usually arrived. A sheathed sword rested against the over-seer's throne. He picked it up and handed it to her.

Lovia had never swung a sword in her life. Somehow she imagined it would be heavier. She would have no trouble gripping the black hilt with both hands, though she suspected it had been made for a man to use one handed. She pulled six inches of the blade free and stared at the dull, black metal.

"Black iron, the finest Hell has to offer. Not even imperial steel can damage it." The overseer settled in his chair. "Go to the rune circle and I'll transport you back."

She did as he bid, clutching the sword to her chest like a little girl with a security blanket.

When the magic tore her apart, she recognized the pain, but it didn't actually hurt. In fact, she'd never experienced anything like the new sensation. Even defining it strained her imagination.

A moment later she found herself in the familiar basement apartment. No light burned, but she had no trouble seeing. Doubtless another of her dubious gifts.

She hurried out of the room and climbed the stairs up to the street. A woman dressed in a filthy smock staggered past, likely drunk off her ass despite the sun being high in the sky. The vagabond took one look at Lovia and screamed.

A powerful desire to silence her flashed through Lovia.

She drew her new sword and swung it hard.

The black blade sliced the woman in half. Overwhelming pleasure washed over Lovia. The most intense she'd ever felt. She looked from the sword to the corpse and back again. Her first kill and instead of feeling sick she felt overjoyed. If warriors felt like this on the battlefield, no wonder so many people joined the legions.

She left the body lying in a slowly expanding pool of blood and hurried deeper into the city. Den Cade Manor waited in Third Circle and she planned to cut a path to her target.

———

Joran rubbed the bridge of his nose as the most recent investigator left the interview room. The square room held only a table and three chairs, one each for Joran and Mia to sit facing whoever they were talking to. He guessed the closet in Alexandra's room had more space. You'd think the palace might find them a nicer place to work, but you'd be wrong.

Since his heart-to-heart with Alexandra, he'd been focused

on putting together the teams they'd need to root out the cultists hiding in their midst. One full team had already been dispatched to Fort Adana to make sure no more vipers lurked in their midst. After that, they'd be doing a tour of the other imperial forts, a task that would likely take most of a year.

The second team still needed two fighters and a second alchemist. The most recent fellow lied no less than five times during the interview, though not about his membership in the cult. Just about pretty much everything else. Not an ideal quality for someone looking for a job finding traitors. Joran feared the man would look the other way for a handful of copper coins.

Mia's hands on his shoulders did wonders to ease the stress. He'd discovered to his considerable delight that she had a gift for massage. Joran tried not to take advantage of his soulmate, but some days he feared he wouldn't have been able to move if she hadn't rubbed down the worst of the cramps.

Who'd have thought that he'd end up achier after a day of interviews than he had after fighting a giant serpent?

"That is amazing, thank you."

"My pleasure." Mia sat in the empty chair beside him. "The better you feel, the better I feel. It's a delightful loop."

Joran nodded. They were still learning things about the soul bond they shared. "How many more do we have to talk to today?"

"Only one more before lunch."

"Thank The One God. Tell him to come back after we eat. I need a break in the worst way."

She smiled and went toward the door. Halfway there it burst open and one of the palace messengers, a boy about thirteen dressed in a crimson tunic, stuck his head in. "Beg pardon, my lord, but Her Majesty requires your presence. It seems there's an emergency in the city."

Joran swallowed a curse. Another emergency, fantastic. They

hadn't had one in week or two. He was starting to get bored. "Where is she?"

"I'll guide you, my lord. This way please."

"I don't suppose she said what sort of emergency?" Joran asked.

"No, my lord." The messenger led them away from the interview room.

Joran hadn't really expected a different answer. No way would Alexandra trust a kid with details.

The veteran fighter waiting outside for his turn to talk to them stared as they hurried off. Mia looked back over her shoulder. "No need to wait. Someone will let you know when the interviews are to resume."

Five minutes of walking and many twists and turns brought them to a closed door. The servants they'd passed on the way showed no particular alarm which made him think that word of the mysterious emergency had yet to spread.

The guide knocked twice, bowed, and took up position ten yards up the hall. Far enough away to make eavesdropping impossible, but close enough to come if called. Someone had trained the young man well. Joran didn't recall interviewing him when he cleared the palace staff, but someone must have otherwise he'd never get this close to Alexandra.

When the door opened, the princess herself stood waiting. She wore her specially prepared crimson cloth armor and had a sword at her hip. Full Iron Princess mode then. Joran would adjust his behavior appropriately.

"More trouble?" he asked.

"Yes, get in here."

Beyond the door he found a meeting room with a large table surrounded by chairs. Two men dressed in crimson uniforms sporting the symbol of a shield crossed with a sword on the chest. City guards, no doubt high-ranking ones, stood in front of their chairs waiting for Alexandra to rejoin them. In the center of the table, someone had spread out a map of the city marked with a number of red X's. No one ever marked anything good with a red X.

The door slammed behind him. Alexandra stomped over to the head of the table and sat, prompting the rest of them to follow suit. "Tell Joran what you told me."

"Yes, Majesty." The older of the two guards, a white-bearded fellow Joran guessed at well over fifty, cleared his throat. "Approximately two hours ago, a woman in First Circle commenced a killing spree. She's already murdered at least twenty civilians that we know about along with fifteen guards that attempted to stop her. We're currently reduced to moving people out of the way as she moves through First Circle. We came to the palace in the desperate hope that someone here would have an idea about how to end her rampage."

"Which is where you come in," Alexandra added.

"Let me get this straight," Mia said. "Fifteen guards failed to take down one woman?"

"You don't understand," the elder guard said. "I saw men run her through, crush her limbs; our archers put a dozen arrows in her. She shrugged them off like they were nothing. The wounds closed instantly. If she feels pain, I saw no sign of it."

"Does the guard have alchemists?" Joran asked.

"Yes, my lord. They tried acid, and poisons of various sorts. None of it worked any better than regular weapons. Alchemist's fire was deemed too dangerous to use in the city."

Certainly a wise precaution. "Does she feel anything?"

"My lord?" the guard asked.

He considered a moment how best to phrase his question. "Does her expression ever change? When you attack does she look angry? Does her speed vary as she walks?"

"Ah, I understand. Yes, her expression does change. When she kills someone with that black sword it looks like..." He glanced at Alexandra and Joran would have sworn he blushed under his beard. "It looks like, um, you know, at the end of an assignation?"

"It looks like she's having an orgasm?" Mia blurted out.

"Yes, ma'am." The older guard looked like he might pass out while his younger companion struggled to hold back sniggers.

"What are you thinking, Joran?" Alexandra asked, seeming neither upset nor amused by the discussion.

"I'm trying to determine if we're dealing with some sort of mindless monster or if she's in any way rational. Has she said anything?"

"No." The elder guard seemed to have himself back under control. "We've tried speaking to her with no results."

"Have you tried binding her?" Joran asked.

"I'm not sure I understand," the guard said.

"I mean take a length of rope or maybe chain since she has a sword, and have a strong man on either end run at her and sweep her off her feet. While she's down, have another group run in and manacle her hands and feet."

"You want to capture her?" Alexandra sounded incredulous.

"It's less a matter of wanting to than a lack of other options. Killing her appears impossible. Or at the very least beyond our current abilities. If the goal is to stop her from causing further havoc, capturing her is our next best option. Once we have her in a controlled environment, study and experimentation may yield the results we seek."

"And if they don't?" Alexandra asked.

"Then wrapping her head to foot in chains and encasing her in cement before transporting her to Oceanus and a ship that will dump her in the middle of the ocean seems a reasonable means of disposal."

Alexandra turned to the guards. "Does that sound doable, gentlemen?"

"We can give it a try, Majesty," the elder guard said. "I won't say it doesn't sound a bit mad, but given our repeated failures, we need to try something."

They stood, bowed, and hurried out the door leaving Joran, Mia, and Alexandra alone with the map. He studied it for a moment, looking at the line of X's. "Anyone have a straightedge?"

Mia drew her sword. "Will this do?"

"I suppose. Lay it along the X's."

She did so and they all leaned closer. Joran followed the edge through the circles before the path reached a familiar point, Den Cade Manor. Could she really be after Joran's family? The one assassin that escaped was a woman. If she'd returned to finish what she started, that would explain her target.

But what had been done to her between now and the original attack?

"She's after my family," Joran said.

"The guards will stop her," Mia said. "Have faith."

Joran smiled, more because of her attempt to reassure him than because he imagined the guards had much hope of success. "I need to get out there, see what's happening with my own eyes."

"It's too dangerous," Alexandra said. "Remember, you're not just another alchemist now, you're a future member of the imperial family."

She sounded like she really cared. That pleased Joran more than he'd expected. "That's kind of you to say, but I think this is exactly the sort of thing your father expects me to handle."

"I don't care what he expects! I want you alive this spring. The One God alone knows who he'll try to marry me off to if you die." A hint of tears glistened in the corners of her eyes. "I want to marry someone I have some hope of loving."

Joran kissed her forehead. "I have no intention of getting close enough for her to harm me. I just want to see her for myself."

"Don't worry, Majesty," Mia said. "I'll keep him safe."

Alexandra shot Mia a hard look. "I'll hold you to that."

Her threat meant nothing when compared to losing your soulmate, but once again Joran appreciated her seemingly genuine concern.

He pushed away from the table. They had a monster to stop, and the sooner the better.

CHAPTER 19

A fifteen-minute run through the city brought Joran and Mia to a cordon of city guards. In Second and Third Circle, you'd never guess an unstoppable monster even now slaughtered her way through First Circle. Third Circle wasn't a surprise. They never cared what happened in First Circle. It might as well be another province as far as they were concerned. Second Circle surprised him more though not as much as it should have.

As they approached, two of the guards, a man and a woman both younger than Joran, raised their hands to stop them.

"This part of the city is off limits," the woman said. "You'll have to turn back."

Joran held up his amulet and the guards' eyes widened. That reaction never got old. "We're from the palace. Do you know where the creature is now?"

"Three blocks west, my lord," the man said. "It's dangerous. I saw that woman, or whatever she is, kill two guards with a single swing of her sword. It cut through them like nothing. She's invincible, like a demon. Our only hope is to flee for the church and pray for The One God to save us, yet even now the guard commander is preparing some other mad plan to try and stop her."

"The mad plan was mine," Joran said. "I'm here to see if it works."

The man blanched. "I meant no offense, my lord."

"Oh, rest assured, I take none. Sometimes a mad plan works where something sensible fails. You can't be afraid to try anything when the situation is desperate. Now, make a path."

The guards shifted aside to let Joran and Mia through. They slowed to a quick walk and two blocks later a familiar stink reached him: Black Bile of the Earth. A moment later they saw her. The creature—and no doubt existed that she'd lost her humanity—appeared slightly melted. Her skin sloughed off in places and numerous black spots showed where she'd been wounded. What remained of her clothes had been reduced to rags. She clutched a sword with an inky black blade that left a trail of dripping blood behind her.

Mia grabbed him and dragged him back into an alley out of sight. "We don't want that thing noticing us."

Joran didn't argue. "That poor woman is filled with Black Bile of the Earth. She's been transformed into a thing that's healed instead of harmed by it. That shouldn't be possible."

A horrendous clanking ended the conversation. A unit of guards came running with a heavy chain between them. Time to see if his crazy idea worked.

Two broad-shouldered men spread out to either side of the street with the chain between them. Four others held manacles.

With a roar, they charged. The chain hung at waist height.

"That's too high," Joran muttered. They were supposed to sweep her feet out from under her.

The woman swung her sword and the black blade sliced through the heavy chain without apparent effort. Even imperial steel didn't cut like that. Nothing Joran had ever heard of did.

When the guards carrying the manacles saw what happened they skidded to a stop and turned to flee.

The woman sprinted forward at a speed even Mia would have had trouble equaling.

She swung the sword. It killed the first guard as easily as it cut through the chain. Her mouth opened and a loud moan emerged. It really did look like killing gave her near-sexual pleasure. Amazing.

"Let's get out of here," Joran said. "I think I know how to stop her."

Mia eagerly led the way down the alley.

"How?" she asked as they turned to make a circle back toward the palace.

"What's the opposite of Black Bile?"

Mia shook her head. "What?"

"A cure all. If she's healed by Black Bile, a cure all should act like poison. That's my theory at least. The hard part will be keeping her still long enough to administer the potion. Eager as she is to kill, we could use bait to lure her into a trap. I can make a powerful adhesive with a short drying time."

"Sure, but who will you use as bait?"

"If this woman is after my family, I bet she'd be eager to sink her sword into me."

Mia stopped, turned to face him, and grabbed both his arms. "That's madness. Do you want to get yourself killed?"

"Of course not, but can I ask someone else to risk themselves to protect my family? Is the life of some random guard less valuable than mine?"

"It is to me," she said with admirable honesty.

"Much as I appreciate your concern, I don't think we have a lot of options. I doubt I could live with myself if I had to order someone to take my place and who'd be stupid enough to volunteer? Besides, I'll have you to back me up."

Mia muttered under her breath as they set out again. Joran had no idea what she said, but doubted it was complimentary.

After a few blocks he said, "Probably best not to mention this to Alexandra until after."

She glanced at him. "You think?"

Joran grinned back. Mia had accepted the plan. He felt it through their link. Working together, he felt certain they could defeat any opponent.

———

M ia crouched under a cloak directly behind Joran. Not quite two hours in the lab yielded a cure all and the four vials she clutched in sweaty hands. As soon as he finished, they hurried back to First Circle. The monstrous woman had made it to within three blocks of Second Circle's gate. A group of reluctant guards had opened it just enough to let them slip under all the while staring and shaking their heads as if believing them doomed. Considering how many people the creature had killed, she had a hard time arguing against their fears.

Only Joran's confidence that his new plan would work had allowed her to put one foot in front of the other. Now here they stood directly in the path of the second-most-lethal creature she'd ever heard of.

"This is such a bad idea," Mia muttered.

"Shh. I don't know how much intellect this thing retains, but I want it to think I'm alone."

"It would have to be completely brain dead to see you standing here and not know it was some kind of a trap." The Black Bile stench reached Mia. "She's coming. Just say when."

"I know. Don't forget to aim for her feet. We want her stuck in place."

"Don't worry, I won't mess up."

"Good, because here she comes."

Mia tensed and shifted one of the vials from her left to her right hand. Aim for her feet, he said. She'll be stuck in place then we can use the other vials to bind her in place, he said. In the safety of the lab it had sounded so simple though she knew even then it wouldn't be.

Her enhanced hearing picked up the thud of footsteps getting rapidly closer.

She gathered herself, ready to spring out from under his oversized cloak.

"Den Cade!" Her voice sounded like the howl of the damned.

"Now, Mia!"

She leapt out, spotted the creature, and threw her vial.

It shattered an instant before her foot struck the ground. A perfect shot even if Mia did say so herself.

The glue wrapped around the creature's bare foot and held her fast. She swung the black sword, missing Joran by inches.

He hastily backed away to a safer distance. "Excellent shot. The other vials, quickly, before she rips her foot off trying to escape."

Now that he mentioned it, the creature was jerking forward with all her might. The flesh around her ankle had already begun to tear.

The second vial shattered against her chest, sticking her offside arm to her body.

The monster swung her black sword, trying to ward off any more vials until she got loose. That argued for some intelligence, but if she was that determined, why not just cut off the stuck foot?

As if reading Mia's mind, she looked down at her bound foot and raised the black sword.

"Her face, quickly," Joran said.

Mia whipped her third vial forward and it smashed across the woman's face. Thick, yellow glue covered her eyes, nose, and mouth. Her thrashing increased tenfold. The arm holding the black sword grazed her face and stuck fast.

Joran shrugged out of his oversized cloak. "Grab an end. We'll put her on her back and stick her to the ground."

Mia pocketed the last vial and took a corner of the cloak. They surged into the mad thing, knocking her backwards. The bones of the bound foot snapped with sickening cracks.

Mia grimaced. She'd seen plenty of horrible things over her many battles, but this had to be one of the worst.

Joran snapped the cloak aside and she threw the final vial. It shattered across her chest and oozed down to the ground. In short order it had hardened, binding the creature in place. She continued to writhe around, trying desperately to get free. At least the glue had sealed her mouth, shutting off the horrendous noises.

"This is a problem," Joran said. "How can I give her the cure all if her mouth is sealed shut?"

"Does it have to go in her mouth?" Mia asked. "You told Her Majesty that she didn't have to swallow it."

"Of course." Joran smacked his forehead. "I'm so used to giving a cure all through the patient's mouth, I totally forgot that this thing isn't a patient. That said, I do need to apply it under her skin. Can I convince you to slice her stomach open so I can pour it in?"

Mia grimaced. "This job is getting more disgusting by the minute. Step back in case anything spurts out."

Joran moved three paces back and she drew her sword. A quick slice opened the creature's skin and black goo oozed out.

He hurried back and poured the cure all. The black stuff dissolved, revealing the flesh underneath.

A moment later the monster started to tremble all over.

Joran grabbed his giant cloak and slung it over the body an instant before it exploded. All the corrupt flesh stayed contained within the cloak.

Mia wiped her forehead. "Is it over?"

"All but the cleanup. I hadn't expected quite that violent of a reaction. We need to collect some guards to keep people away from this spot then we need to try and figure out where she came from. If more of those things can show up the same way, we'd be in trouble."

"That's putting it mildly." Mia toed the cloak aside enough to poke the black sword out. "I think I'll take this. It's definitely an upgrade on my current sword."

"We wouldn't want it falling into the wrong hands either."

Mia touched the hilt and immediately jerked her hand back. "It burned me."

Joran hurried over. "Let me see."

She held out her hand. Both fingers that had touched the hilt were an ugly, blistered red. "We made it through the fight without a mark and now I get singed just from a touch of the hilt. What are the odds?"

"Poor, I'd say. Don't worry, I have something in my kit I can treat this with, but I left it back in the lab so it wouldn't slow me down. I wonder if only someone transformed the way she'd been can touch it safely. We can get some tongs before we return. Come on, let's find those guards then get you fixed up."

CHAPTER 20

After receiving many congratulations and slaps on the back from the city guards, Joran and Mia returned to the palace and headed straight for Cordius's and now Joran's lab. The servants had fully stocked the room with a fresh batch of chemicals and reagents. Joran's kit waited right where he'd left it. He dug out a paste designed to heal burns and applied a thin layer of healing paste to Mia's reddened fingers.

The skin instantly absorbed the paste and turned back to a healthy bronze. He'd done his best not to let his worries show through their link, but since he'd never seen anything like that sword, he hadn't been totally certain the usual methods would suffice to heal the damage. Despite the fact that it looked like a burn, neither flame nor acid had caused the damage.

In fact, he wasn't entirely certain how the sword's hilt had hurt Mia. He suspected that an application of revealing powder would show fairly strong magic. What sort of magic and how the unfortunate woman came to possess it were yet more in a long line of mysteries he needed to solve. But not the most pressing at the moment.

"Better?"

She nodded. "Much, thanks."

"Good." He shouldered his kit. "We'd best get back out there and try to track her back to her point of origin."

"Maybe dinner first?"

Joran grinned. "Excellent idea. Especially since we skipped lunch."

"I'm glad we did." Mia hopped down off his workbench. "Seeing what happened to that woman when she died turned my stomach. I've never seen anything like it, have you?"

"No, and I'd be perfectly happy to never see it again."

The door slammed open and Alexandra strode in. "I've received word from the city watch that you dealt with the invincible monster without help from their soldiers. Why is it I'm getting this report from the guard captain and not my fiancé?"

"Mia was injured and we came straight here so I could heal her. You were my next stop." Joran did his best to look sincere. "I didn't think the guards would send word so quickly."

"They were very impressed that the two of you handled a threat that took the lives of nearly thirty of their fellows on your own. This is getting to be a habit." She hugged him. "I'm glad you're okay. Both of you."

"It's easier to deal with a threat when you understand it. I regret that it cost so many lives before I figured it out."

"Soldiers die all the time," Alexandra said. "It's unfortunate, but also part of the job."

"I suppose so. Mia and I were discussing dinner before heading back out to trace the monster's origin. Would you like to join us?"

"I'd like that very much. We can have it brought to our suite and while we're waiting you can tell me all about the battle."

Joran really didn't want to tell her about acting as bait, but he also didn't want to get in the habit of lying to his future wife. That sort of habit might be hard to break.

They made the walk to Alexandra's suite in silence. She held his hand and Mia stayed a step behind them. Joran hated making her walk anywhere but at his side, but he sensed no resentment. Instead, she seemed pleased that he and Alexandra were getting along. Probably hoping they'd end up in bed so she could enjoy a psychic threesome. Joran held out little hope for that with all they had to do.

At last, they settled in the living room while a servant set out for the kitchen. When only the three of them remained Joran told her everything, even the bait part.

"I don't know where she came from or how she ended up as she did, but I am almost certain this was the woman that escaped after the attack on my family. Nothing else would explain why she made a beeline for the manor or how she recognized me. My name was the only coherent thing she said during the entire encounter."

"How could you do something so reckless?" she demanded when he'd finished the story. "You know how important you are to the empire. Your life is worth ten thousand ordinary soldiers."

"I doubt their families would agree. Much like with the serpent, Mia and I were the best ones to deal with the creature. I won't deny the risk, but I also refuse to put people in danger when they have no hope of winning. It worked out in the end."

"This time, but what about next time?"

Joran shook his head and swallowed a sigh. "Whatever we're dealing with is big. A threat unlike any the empire has ever faced. We can't win if we take no risks. By The One God, I sound like my father. Anyway, hearing reports and making suggestions is one thing, but I need to see what I'm dealing with firsthand to figure out how to handle it. It's just the way my mind works."

"I don't like it." Alexandra crossed her arms then turned to look at Mia. "You're his soulmate, can't you make him avoid this kind of crazy thing?"

"I tried, but I can also feel through our link when he really needs what he says he needs. I fear we both have to accept that this is the way it is."

Alexandra muttered something about stupid geniuses, but thankfully the servant returned with their meal before she had a chance to make another argument. And thank The One God for that. He had a hard enough time doing what he had to without needing to justify every decision to Alexandra.

They ate roast chicken and root vegetables while sipping wine. The food and rest did wonders for Joran and when he'd cleaned his plate he said, "Delicious. My compliments to the palace chef."

Alexandra smiled. "I'm glad none of the kitchen staff turned out to be traitors. You're going back out?"

"Afraid so. The longer we wait, the harder it'll be to track her. Only an exceedingly empty stomach convinced me to take this long." He turned to Mia. "Ready?"

She stood and adjusted her sword. "As I'll ever be."

———

Only a couple hours of light remained when Joran and Mia left the palace and retraced their steps to First Circle. Far from ideal, but like he'd told Alexandra, Joran didn't want to waste any time on the off chance more creatures like that one showed up. Beside him, Mia carried a pair of smith's tongs and a length of heavy canvas. He hoped that by avoiding direct contact with bare skin, they might avoid getting burned. If not, he didn't know how they'd move the sword somewhere safe.

"I really hope we find whatever we're looking for before dark," Mia said.

She probably didn't even need the link to know he'd been thinking the exact same thing. "Shouldn't take too long. I memorized the map so if we follow the X's we'll end up at her starting point. Hopefully, anyway. If she didn't kill anyone for a few blocks, that will complicate things."

"You have a wonderful gift for understatement."

This time of day, the streets in Third Circle were busy with the rich and powerful out for an evening stroll, no doubt blissfully unaware of how many people died a few hours ago. Sometimes Joran envied them their arrogance and ignorance. He hadn't been much better when he'd been focused on his research to the exclusion of all else. That felt like a lifetime ago. Or maybe a dream.

He asked himself now and then if he'd go back to his old life if given the opportunity. Part of him, a large part, wouldn't mind foisting his problems off on someone else. Another, larger part, recognized that he had something important to offer. He also understood that if the empire fell, his old life wouldn't exist.

"You're thinking really hard," Mia said. "I can almost hear the gears turning in your brain."

"Sorry, walking through the old neighborhood made me think of my life before I left for Stello Province. It's hard to believe how much things have changed in a few months. Would you believe that no one had ever tried to kill me before those lizardmen at the site of Alexandra's crash?"

"You handled yourself well."

The guards let them out into Second Circle without questions.

"Father's training kicked in. Without that, I'd have been frozen stiff with fear."

Second Circle had even more traffic than Third as everyone made their way home from whatever job they worked. The pair walked in comfortable silence until they reached the gate to

First Circle. The guards had opened the portcullis back up and when they spotted Joran and Mia offered friendly waves.

"Our popularity has increased," Mia said. "They never thought that much of me when I actually served in the guard."

"Why? You're smart and incredibly talented. I would have thought they'd have fought to keep you from joining the Iron Guard."

"I had a bit of a bad attitude at the time. When you see how the guards treat people from First Circle versus those from Third, it reminds you how unfair the empire can be. As a First Circle orphan, I sometimes let my personal thoughts shine through a little too brightly."

Joran had no trouble imagining that. "If you felt that strongly, I'm surprised you agreed to go with Alexandra."

"She was so beautiful and no one of importance had ever seen anything of value in me before her." Mia frowned. "Did she use that fact to manipulate me into greater loyalty?"

"Did she know about it?"

"No idea."

"Then I don't know, but I can assure you that if she did, Alexandra wouldn't have thought twice about using your past to control you. She wouldn't have been able to help herself. A lifetime of training would have her doing it before she even thought about what her actions meant. Here we are."

Ahead of them a squad of ten guards stood around the remains of the creature—Joran refused to think of her as human. They looked bored, leaning on their spears and chatting. Aside from the smell, it looked like easy duty.

As soon as they spotted Joran and Mia approaching, they hastened to straighten up and look as if they cared about their task. Joran didn't especially care about their alertness as long as their presence kept everyone away. The remains were likely toxic and he didn't want anyone or anything touching them or the sword.

"Any trouble?" Joran asked.

"No, my lord," one of the guards said. "Some of the locals stopped to stare, but no one tried anything. How long are we going to have to guard this spot?"

"Until I figure out a way to clean it up without getting some poor slave killed in the process. Or worse, have them end up transformed into another monster."

The guards all muttered at that. The last thing anyone wanted was another of those monsters wandering the city.

"We'll make sure everyone keeps their distance," the spokesman assured him, now sounding a good deal more focused.

"Good." Joran pulled out a pouch of revealing powder and sprinkled it on the sword.

As he expected, it flashed, indicating magic, strong magic too. Not as powerful as the ritual that Samaritan used to wake the serpent, but after that, it was the strongest he'd ever seen. Joran shook his head. He knew how to make an oil that turned a sword magical, enhancing both its sharpness and durability, for about ten minutes, but compared to this enchantment, his oil might as well have been water.

"Should we wrap it up now?" Mia asked.

Joran debated a moment. If anyone wanted to steal the sword, they'd be basically gift wrapping it for them. But surrounded as it was by guards, the risk should be minimal. "Yeah, let's see if we can pick it up wrapped."

He took the canvas and Mia gripped the tongs in both hands. Gingerly, she clamped onto the flat of the blade and lifted it off the ground. "So far so good."

Joran slid the canvas under the sword and she laid it back down. He folded one side over and touched the sword through the canvas.

No reaction. Good, it looked safe enough to move it. Maybe

a leather worker could make Mia some heavy-duty gloves. That would let her wield the sword safely.

They finished wrapping it, nodded to the guards, and set out. The bloodstains on the cobblestones made it easy to follow the monster's path. About a block from their final encounter, he spotted something black mixed in among the blood. Had some of the Black Bile leaked out of her? That would certainly complicate the cleanup.

He sniffed but didn't get the distinct odor. Might be something else, but he had no idea what. Setting that aside for future consideration, they moved on.

Most of half an hour later they reached a body lying in two pieces across from a rundown tenement. The door to the basement apartment stood open.

Mia drew her sword. "I can smell Black Bile inside. This is the place."

Joran pulled a light vial from his kit and shook it until a bright blue glow emerged. He took a step and Mia immediately moved in front of him. "Better let me go first."

He couldn't exactly argue. If anything nasty remained inside, she would certainly be better able to handle it than him. Just to be safe he grabbed one of the adhesive vials and held it in his other hand. If they had to run, that would buy them a little time.

They stepped into a rather unimpressive kitchen that didn't look like it had been used for as long as Joran had been alive. It took only a minute to confirm that the apartment was empty. The only thing of interest, a circle marked by strange symbols, sat on the floor of the apartment's lone bedroom.

Mia sheathed her sword. "Well that turned out kind of anticlimactic. Not that I'm complaining. I had no interest in fighting another one of those things."

"You said it." Joran replaced the adhesive vial and dug the pouch of revealing powder out of his kit. A sprinkle of powder across the markings set off a flash nearly as bright as the sword.

"Great, more powerful magic of unknown purpose. Could you hold the light for a moment?"

Mia took it and Joran pulled out his workbook and a charcoal pencil. With deft strokes he copied the markings for future study. The pile of "things for future study" just kept growing and he had little hope of catching up soon.

"We'll need another squad of guards to keep an eye on this place," he said. "The residents won't be pleased, but we should also evacuate the building."

"Is that absolutely necessary?" Mia handed him the light vial. "If you make them leave, the people here will have nowhere else to go. Most will end up on the street."

Joran grimaced. "Good point. For safety reasons, I'd like the building empty, but having people on the streets isn't an ideal result. Maybe we can set the guards to watching and if anything happens, they can warn the residents to flee. The risk is higher, but it would let them stay in their homes."

"I think that's the best option. When I lived on the streets, you had to keep one eye open all the time. Having four walls and a door makes a big difference."

He nodded, more than happy to let her take the lead on this matter. "Let's make the arrangements and call it a night. I'm beat."

"I like that plan. After all, we need to be well rested for whatever monster we need to fight tomorrow."

Joran smiled at her joke but inside his soul wept. The way things had been going, that might well happen.

CHAPTER 21

J oran slammed the book he'd been reading shut. The author boasted that it contained a sample of every written language the empire had encountered and he'd updated it only a year ago. Yet Joran found nothing even close to the markings he and Mia saw in the dark basement apartment. Clearly someone had encountered it, yet no mention of it existed in any of the books where he'd expected to find it.

Ordinarily he loved visiting the imperial library, but today he got only frustration for his efforts. He and Mia arrived not long after breakfast and he'd settled in to read. Mia had offered to help, but half an hour of reading the dry historical texts had her fast asleep. Joran envied her. For all he'd accomplished, he might as well have taken a nap too.

No, that wasn't completely true. He had eliminated a few sources which helped to narrow his search. He smiled at himself. If that didn't sound delusional, he didn't know what might.

"Joran," a soft, familiar voice said.

He turned to find Julian tiptoeing toward him. He hadn't been to see his friend since his return from Stello Province. Not terribly thoughtful, but then given all that had happened, he supposed something had to give.

He eased away from the desk where Mia slept and joined Julian between two of the bookcases. "Julian. Sorry I didn't find you sooner. How are things?"

"Amazing. Catia and I got engaged two weeks ago. And speaking of engagements, I heard you were going to marry Princess Alexandra. How did that happen? And why are you here with another woman? Won't she be mad?"

Joran smiled at Julian's enthusiasm. "The other woman is Mia Amino Den Cade. She's my soulmate and adopted sister. Alexandra knows we're here together and she's not jealous or mad. As for my engagement, I saved Alexandra's life twice in Stello Province. Her father thought that meant I should marry her. No one consulted me on the decision. That said, I've come to both like and respect the princess. Who knows, by spring, maybe we'll even love each other. Stranger things have happened."

He'd received strict instructions to make no mention of the emperor's near-death experience or his part in warding it off. As far as anyone knew, the emperor had been under the weather and taking a rest from his many duties to recover.

"A soulmate and a wife," Julian said. "That's amazing. And you didn't even want to go."

"The trip turned out better than I'd dared hope, no doubt about that. What about you? You and Catia must have really hit it off if you're engaged already."

"She's wonderful." Julian sounded almost delirious as he spoke. "Sweet, funny, smart, pretty. I don't know how I got so lucky, but I thank The One God every morning that I asked her to that vivisection months ago. Anyway, can I help you with anything?"

"I don't know. Take a look at this." They returned to the table and Joran showed him the runes. He'd copied them in ink so they wouldn't smudge. "Ever seen anything like them?"

Julian shook his head. "Never. Where did you find them?"

A slum in First Circle seemed an unwise reply so he said, "A cave the natives of Stello Province considered holy. The design is completely different from the pictographs they use for written communication."

"Wow. You should write a monograph and submit it to the library. I bet they'd like to have it for their collection."

Joran chuckled. As if he'd have time for that anytime soon. "We'll see. Any thoughts about where else I might look? Maybe the Forbidden Section?"

Julian looked all around as if afraid someone might have heard his suggestion. "I don't know what's there. No one outside the church does. I'm not even sure how you'd get permission."

"I figured I'd get a letter from my future father-in-law. I'm pretty sure no one would be dumb enough to refuse someone with an imperial writ."

"Probably not, but I'd advise against the Forbidden Section unless all other avenues fail." A soft bell sounded from the front of the library. "I have to go. Do you still want to get dinner with Catia and me sometime?"

"Sure. Maybe I can convince Alexandra to join us. Like a double date." Julian paled and Joran had to swallow a laugh. "She doesn't bite."

"Of course not. See you later." Julian hurried away.

Joran shook his head and sat beside Mia.

"I like how proud you sound when you call me your sister," she said.

"Are you just pretending to sleep so you don't have to read?"

She opened one eye and looked up at him. "Do you think I'd do something like that?"

"I do now. Not that it matters. I've checked every relevant

book and there's nothing about the marks. Considering how much Black Bile had been injected into that woman, I think our next stop has to be the fort where it bubbles up. There must be an alchemist stationed there and I can't imagine anyone else knowing more."

Mia pushed away from the desk and stood. "Anything's better than sitting here trying to force myself to read those books. They must have been written by the most boring people on the planet."

"We prefer to call such books dry."

"Wine is dry. Wits can be dry. This—" she tapped the cover of the book she'd read for twenty minutes "—is a cure for insomnia. That you kept at it for hours may be the most impressive feat I've ever seen."

Joran didn't point out that he often spent whole days tweaking a formula until he got it perfect. Reading, even boring reading, didn't begin to compare.

"Do you know where the fort is?" he asked.

"No. Don't you?"

Joran shook his head. He didn't even know what they named the place. Should be easy enough to find. Maybe he could borrow a dragon ship to make the trip even faster.

After all he'd been through, the thought didn't even terrify him, though he certainly intended to check it thoroughly for bombs.

CHAPTER 22

Antius lost all track of time as he and the trackers rode northeast. The days all ran together. They travelled from sunup to sunset, ate in the saddle, and slept in rotation so nothing snuck up on them. Even a day out from Tiber they followed this routine and he wholly approved. The more he saw of his guides, the more Antius felt confident that they actually had the knowledge and skills to help him find Bellator. He really shouldn't have doubted. The pope wouldn't deal with just anyone. His Holiness selected only the finest servants. It shamed Antius to admit he'd doubted that.

Yesterday they crossed out of the empire, passing a border fort in the early afternoon without pausing. The soldiers on duty watched them without calling out. No one cared if you left the empire and Antius doubted the guards at least would care if they returned. The worst part of leaving the empire was the lack of roads. They'd found a rough trail that went generally northeast and followed that until dark.

Now even the trail had vanished, and Trupo simply picked a path between the trees. Shrill squawks of birds filled the air, but compared to the southern jungle, the northern forest stayed quiet. Antius would have preferred more noise to distract him from memories of Bellator. It still strained his belief to think that the most devout worshipper he'd ever known had betrayed everything they'd believed in.

"How long until we reach our destination?" Antius asked when they paused to let Trupo consider the path forward.

"Another week will get us to the last place we saw signs of Bellator," Trupo said. "From there, the real search begins."

"What's the terrain like?" Antius asked.

"Rough. There's a sunken area with sheer cliffs. It looks like a giant, nearly round footprint about three hundred feet deep." Trupo looked back at him. "I saw Bellator fall off that cliff. His Holiness says the man survived. I believe someone else found his gear and took up the mantel of a White Knight. Whatever the case, our hope is to find some sign of what happened at the bottom of the cliff."

Trupo set out again. What he'd described sounded impossible, but then again, if you'd asked Antius if a giant black serpent big enough to crush the walls of Cularo like a petulant child smashing a block tower existed, he'd have said you were mad.

Nothing troubled the group as they traveled through the forest. Antius actually found it quite peaceful. They hadn't seen a single predator, much less a monster. He had trouble imagining why the empire hadn't expanded to encompass this part of the continent. The legions wouldn't even have to bring a restive population to heel. The forests were rich with timber and game. Everything he'd seen indicated that this would make an ideal province.

Six days later, nothing had changed his mind. Outside of the capital, he'd never felt as safe as he did riding through the forest. They emerged from the tree line in the early afternoon. Directly ahead of them lay the sunken area Trupo mentioned.

Antius stared, his mouth hanging open. He'd never seen

anything like the giant sinkhole. It had to measure several miles across.

"By The One God." He made the circle over his heart.

"Impressive, isn't it?" Trupo asked. "We'll make camp well back from the edge and descend at first light. Big as it is, I doubt we'll need more than a few days to search the area."

"You sound dubious that we'll find anything," Antius said.

Trupo shrugged. "There's nothing around here for days, maybe weeks, in every direction. If, by some miracle, Bellator did survive, why would he hang around? My only hope, and it's a faint hope, is that we find some obvious way a person might get out of the sinkhole other than climbing the cliff, which, without ropes, is impossible. If we find that path, then we'll have a direction for our hunt."

"And if we don't?" Antius asked.

Trupo shrugged again. "Then we climb back up and expand the search north and east. If there's anything to find, we'll find it."

Antius liked the man's dedication if not his level of enthusiasm.

———

Antius's eagerness to continue the search led to a fitful night's sleep. As soon as the sun colored the horizon he rose, eager to begin their descent. To his considerable disappointment, the trackers showed no such enthusiasm. They lounged around the grassy patch where they'd made camp and the biggest man in the group, a nearly seven-foot-tall giant with a shaved head and a sword so big Antius doubted he'd be able to lift it with both hands, fixed breakfast.

For his part, Trupo got busy checking his weapons. Antius stalked over. "What's the delay? Today might be the day we solve the mystery of what happened to Bellator. We should set the ropes and climb down at once."

Trupo shook his head. "Too early. The sun won't reach all the way to the bottom of the sinkhole for another couple hours. We don't want to be stumbling around down there in the dark. While I doubt anything dangerous lives in the hole, I don't know that for sure. When in doubt, assume there's danger and act accordingly. Caution never got anyone killed. If you need something to occupy yourself, you can help Helena check the ropes."

The two hours he spent with the group's sole female member looking for frayed sections of rope felt longer than the entire ride north. It didn't help that she hardly spoke a word as they worked, seeming wholly focused on the task in front of her. Knowing that the ropes would be the only thing between her and a rapid descent probably did wonders to focus her mind.

Pity it did nothing to help Antius. He knew in his heart and soul that they'd find the truth at the bottom of the hole. Perhaps The One God spoke directly to him. He liked to believe that, but didn't think so much of his importance. No, this feeling came from inside not out.

At last, they set out for the cliff's edge. The horses were left to wander and graze unbound. Trupo assured him that they'd been well trained and would come when called. Antius hoped so as he had no desire to walk all the way back to Tiber. That said, he saw the necessity of letting them graze as they might be days exploring the pit.

At the edge, Antius looked down into the hole. Trees grew thick and healthy. It looked like a section of the forest had fallen straight down. He tried to imagine how that might have happened and failed. Only an act of The One God seemed possible.

Trupo directed his team to tie the ropes off to massive boulders jutting up a few yards back from the edge. No need to worry about them coming free of the earth as they climbed down. Next, supplies were lowed at the end of the three ropes.

Once they reached the bottom of the hole Trupo said, "Helena and Cartus will descend with me to secure our landing point. Only when we've reached the bottom will the rest of you start your climb. Understood?"

Trupo aimed that last question directly at Antius. Eager as he was to reach the bottom, Antius fully appreciated the precautions needed for this sort of mission.

"I understand," Antius said. "Now can we get started?"

Trupo offered a humorless smile, reached for the center rope, and eased himself over the edge. The climb down took most of half an hour, but at last a shout came from below. "We're clear and the area is secure. Begin your descent."

Antius needed no more urging. He started immediately down the center rope. He'd gone about twenty yards when a crunch from above brought him to a halt. He looked up. Looking back down at him stood a figure in a white cloak, his face obscured by a raised hood.

"Bellator!"

The figure gave a shake of his head. "Antius. I am sorry to see the pope sent you to join his merry band of killers. You are, perhaps, the one White Knight I regret having to kill."

Light flashed on a blade and Antius suddenly found himself weightless and dropping like a rock.

Thinking fast, he grabbed the hem of his cloak and pulled it tight. That slowed his fall a fraction and dragged him deeper into the hole.

He aimed for a branch in the crown of the tallest tree.

The impact drove the air out of him, but somehow he held on. Grunting with a mix of pain and exertion, he pulled himself up onto the branch. Just in time to watch one of the trackers fall past him to land hard enough to make an impression in the dirt. Blood exploded out of the body and Antius had to look away.

But for The One God's grace and his alchemically enhanced cloak, that certainly would have been his fate.

Trupo strode into sight and looked up at him. "You okay?"

"I'm alive. Everything hurts too much for it to be otherwise. I'll join you in a moment."

A moment turned out to be closer to ten minutes as he picked his way gingerly down the tree. He hadn't been climbing since his youth and had no desire to resume the hobby. His knees wobbled when his feet finally touched the ground. He made a circle over his heart. He'd survived, for the moment anyway.

"Seems I was wrong," Trupo said. "Bellator survived after all. But more importantly, how did he find us?"

"I wish I knew. I hate to think someone in the church warned him. It's possible someone saw us leaving along with our direction of travel and guessed our destination." Antius shook his head. "I just don't know. My condolences for the loss of your friends."

"Thank you. We all know this is a dangerous job, but no one expects to go out like that." Neither of them looked back at the mangled corpses as they walked to rejoin the other survivors.

"What's important now," Trupo said when they reached Helena and the other tracker, Cartus. "Is finding a way out of this hole. If Bellator found a way to escape, then we can as well."

"When I catch up to him," Helena said. "I'm going to gut him like a fish."

Antius cocked his head. "Bellator said something before cutting the rope. He said you were the pope's merry band of killers. I thought you were trackers."

"We are whatever His Holiness needs us to be," Trupo said. "When the pope gives you a mission, you don't quibble over exact details. Now let's get to work. I'd like to be out of here before dark."

Antius grimaced at Trupo's nonanswer. Someone was leading him astray. Odd that he considered the man that tried to kill him more likely to be telling him the truth than the companions he'd have to trust to get him safely out of this place.

CHAPTER 23

Joran once again found himself seated on the couch beside Alexandra in her luxurious palace suite. The princess looked lovely in her informal blue robes. Life would be so much easier if he only needed to stare at her for the rest of his days. More pleasant too. Circumstances, unfortunately, dictated he move on.

He'd made several more fruitless visits to the imperial library just to make sure he'd missed nothing. He hadn't. And Mia made it abundantly clear that she'd spent all the time in the library she wanted to. No, it was time to take the next step and travel to the fort where the army secured the Black Bile spring.

"Let me get this straight," Alexandra said. "You want to travel to the Black Bile spring so you can talk to the alchemist serving at Fort Death in the hope that he knows more about the nasty stuff than you do. They don't experiment with the poison. The garrison's job is simply to prevent anyone from gaining access."

"I'm out of ideas," Joran said. "I've exhausted all my avenues of inquiry save for the fort and the Forbidden Section of the library. And, frankly, I'd prefer to try the fort than ask your father for permission to enter that area. Avoiding the church's attention, at least until we have a better handle on the situation, seems prudent to me."

"Me too." She sounded less than thrilled to admit that fact. "Okay, you can go, but take the new investigation unit with you. They need to get started sometime and a little extra muscle never hurt anything."

Joran would happily take all the help he could get. "Do I need a letter of introduction or something?"

"No. Your amulet entitles you to access any location not directly under imperial family control. Though I wouldn't try and use it to enter any sensitive church sites."

Joran cocked his head. "The church has sensitive sites?"

"You mentioned one of them a moment ago, the Forbidden Section of the library. I think having books no one can read is stupid, but the church deems the information too valuable to destroy and too dangerous for general consumption." She shrugged. "Father deemed it not worth the argument to fight them over access. Anyway, like any large organization, the church has its secrets."

The idea of the church keeping secrets from the imperial family didn't sit well with Joran, but he had no say in the matter and wanted none. He had enough on his plate without sticking his nose further into politics.

"You will be careful, won't you?"

"Of course I will."

She kissed him. "A little something to remind you why you need to return safe and sound."

He needed no reminders, but would take all she had to offer. "What about a dragon ship?"

"Sorry. Fort Death doesn't have a big enough yard for you to land. Besides, we don't want to draw any more attention to your visit than necessary."

"I suppose not. Where is the fort anyway?"

"Southwest, only about three days' ride from Tiber."

Joran shuddered. Having that much liquid evil so close to the imperial capital struck him as a horrible idea. Not that they had any way to move the spring.

"Mia's getting impatient. I'll see you in a week or so."

Alexandra nodded. "This might be the first time I've said this to anyone besides my brother, but I'll miss you."

Joran smiled, surprised to find he felt the same.

———

The road to Fort Death wound through the imperial homeland. They passed scores of wagons bringing fall food to the capital. Everyone smiled and waved at Joran and his companions, seeming happy and utterly unaware of how deep the empire's troubles ran.

That suited Joran fine. He had hoped to keep the danger contained and away from the ordinary citizens.

The damage Cularo had taken during both the lizardman raid and the serpent's attack had been bad enough. They needed no more civilian deaths, especially in the homeland. If anything major happened here, it would rattle the empire to its core.

Even the bright, clear weather made him feel like the world wanted everything to be okay. Madness, of course. The world cared nothing for their problems or their successes. Sometimes he wondered if The One God himself cared. If the priests had any idea what they were talking about, he was supposed to be a benevolent deity that loved his children. If that were true, you'd think zapping any giant monsters that popped up would be the least he could do.

Joran glanced at Mia who rode beside him. She looked much more comfortable on a horse with a saddle and reins. Her gaze darted from one side of the road to the other, her hand never staying far from the hilt of her sword. As long as she didn't have to read, her focus never wavered. Behind them rode the ten-person investigation team. They all had at least a dozen years' experience and had passed his loyalty tests. All were eager to bring any enemy of the empire to justice.

Over the past couple nights, Joran had spoken to the unit commander, Caeso. The man had served in the Second Legion for eight years before transferring to the scout corps. From there he served for a year on the front lines north of Stello Province. A serious injury earned him a medal and a place in the inspector general's office.

He struck Joran as smart and determined, a good combination for the tasks ahead. He also had no living family. Another good thing for the tasks ahead.

A smaller road leading west branched off the main southern road. It led directly past Fort Death. Not that most people had any idea about the fort's purpose. It looked exactly the same as every other imperial fort and the guards mounted patrols to make sure nothing happened on the nearby roads.

Joran frowned and turned to Mia. "Did you notice any patrols for the last day or so? I've been thinking so much about the Black Bile I can't even remember."

"No, why?"

"Well, the fort is supposed to send out regular patrols as part of their cover. Since we haven't run into a single soldier, I can't help thinking perhaps something's wrong."

"I thought we'd pretty well established that something was wrong," Mia said.

"In general, yes, but I had no particular concerns about Fort Death. Did you?"

"Not really, though I hadn't given it a ton of thought. We're over a hundred miles away from the library and that's all that interested me."

"Is all well, Lord Den Cade?" Caeso asked.

Joran looked back at the handsome imperial. With his

perfect bronze skin and chiseled features, Caeso should have gotten work in recruitment. He'd be ideal.

"We were just discussing the apparent lack of local patrols. Have you noticed anything we might have missed?"

"No, my lord, though given how peaceful the homeland is, perhaps they deemed the patrols a waste of effort."

"It's hardly up to the fort commander to decide that sort of thing. The patrols are what keep the homeland peaceful and show the people that the empire is working hard to protect them. If you're correct, we may need to arrange a new commander."

"We'll find out soon enough," Mia said.

Joran turned back to find the walls of Fort Death looming directly ahead. He didn't know exactly what he'd expected. Somehow the place looked too ordinary given the importance of its task. The wooden walls were topped with sharpened stakes that protected the battlements. A guard tower at each corner provided a clear field of view for the archers. The top floor of the keep rose above the wall and a crimson flag with a golden eagle flew over it.

Mia ripped her sword from its sheath.

"What?" Joran asked.

"Where are the guards? The walls and towers look abandoned."

Now that she mentioned it he noticed the same thing. Missing patrols were one thing, but leaving the battlements unguarded? No imperial commander competent enough to earn a position leading a fort would allow that. Something had clearly gone wrong.

Now they needed to find out what.

"Orders, Lady Den Cade?" Caeso asked.

"Dismount and leave the horses a safe distance from the walls," Mia said. "Hopefully the gate is unlocked. If not, we'll need to send someone over the wall."

Joran allowed himself a slight smile despite the situation. Mia still felt uneasy being called Lady Den Cade even though, as his adopted sister, she deserved the title. At least she remembered to answer when addressed with her honorific.

The group dismounted and one of the investigators got the job of staying behind with the horses. Whether that ended up being a good assignment or a bad one, time would tell.

Everyone had their weapons out as they approached the heavy gate. The foot-thick double doors looked heavy enough to withstand at least a few blows from a battering ram. Though if an enemy made it this far into the empire, they'd all be in serious trouble.

Mia pushed hard on the doors. They rattled but showed no sign of moving. "The bar's up. I need four volunteers to climb the wall and open the gate."

Every one of the investigators raised their hand. Nothing like a new post to increase enthusiasm. No doubt in six months they'd all know better.

Caeso picked four and two ropes ending in iron grappling hooks were tossed up and over the wall. Joran had thought Mia'd lost her mind when he saw the ropes in their gear, but it seemed she'd been wise to bring them.

The chosen four went hand over hand up and over the wall. When they disappeared into the training yard Joran listened hard for anything that might give him a clue to what was going on in the fort.

Aside from the soldiers' scuffing footsteps he heard nothing. Half a minute later the gate rattled and the bar crashed to the ground. When the gate finally opened it revealed only an empty yard, the main keep, and two outbuildings that all looked as empty as the rest of the fort. No bodies, no signs of battle, nothing to indicate why no one still patrolled the walls.

"Did they abandon their posts?" Mia asked.

"The entire fort and none of them came to Tiber to report

what happened?" Joran asked. "Doubtful. Besides, who put the bar back up?"

"Certainly no one was killed here," Mia countered.

He had no argument for that. If someone received a major wound, there'd be a dark spot in the dirt where the blood spilled.

"Should we fan out and search?" Caeso asked.

"No," Mia said. "We stick together. I won't have any stragglers picked off."

Mia led them toward the nearest of the two outbuildings. Joran slipped a vial of adhesive out of his kit. Just in case he panicked and hit someone on their side, at least the adhesive wouldn't kill them. In his other hand he held a blue light vial.

When they reached the door, he shook it until the light burned bright.

Mia kicked the door in and he raised the light. Nothing but a blacksmith shop with a cold forge. The tools all hung from hooks along the wall, untouched and forgotten. Even if the soldiers all deserted, no smith would leave without his tools.

The group moved on to the second outbuilding. This one held a collection of tools for repairing and maintaining the fort. Still no people or even bodies.

That left the keep itself.

"I'm not well versed on army protocol," Joran said. "Does the commander not have to send regular reports to some general or prefect or something?"

"Reports are supposed to go out quarterly," Caeso said. "But they don't get read at once and assuming no one led with, 'Everyone in the fort vanished,' the commander's immediate superior probably just skimmed the report and filed it somewhere."

"Great. Good to know everyone's on their game. Mia, remind me to pay a visit to whoever's in charge of this place when we get back. If anyone noticed anything weird going on, I'd like to see what they observed."

"Sure. Do we check the keep?" Mia asked.

"Yes. The bile spring is in the basement. We need to see if anyone's accessed it. With no one guarding the cursed thing for The One God alone knows how long, anyone might have waltzed in here and helped themselves to as much poison as they wanted."

"Someone like Samaritan."

Joran nodded. "Exactly like Samaritan. Or whoever gave Cordius his vial."

Mia scowled and her eyebrows drew down as she led them to the keep. The door hung slightly askew, like someone forced it open. It was the first sign of violence Joran had seen since they arrived.

Using the tip of her sword, Mia nudged the door open. The entry sat dark and empty, the torches in the wall sconces long since used up. Still no sign of violence beyond the damaged door. The first and second floors were as empty as the rest of the fort.

Only the basement and the bile spring remained to check. Joran's stomach twisted as he followed Mia to the stairs down. If the poison hung as thick in the air as he feared, just breathing without protection might be enough to kill them.

"Just a moment," Joran said when they reached the basement door. He dug out a treated face covering and handed it to Mia. "Tie that around your nose and mouth. Don't remove it until we get back upstairs. Caeso, you and your people will have to stay up here. I only have the two cloths. Keep well back from the door."

"Yes, my lord," Caeso said. "Please be careful. I don't want to have to tell Her Majesty that something happened to you."

Joran grinned behind his face covering. "Don't worry, I'm sure she'd make your execution painless."

Caeso paled.

"I'm kidding. Relax, I'm sure the basement is as empty as the rest of this place. As soon as we figure out whether the bile spring has been disturbed, we'll head back to the capital."

Joran held the blue light over his head and Mia led the way downstairs. They stepped onto the dirt floor and he looked around. Not much to see really. Looked like they kept nothing down here. No doubt keeping equipment in a space filled with miasma would be a pain whenever they needed something.

"Where's the spring?" Mia asked.

"Toward the rear wall. See the black lines running through the floor? That's the bile, poisoning the dirt. The toxicity is absolutely amazing."

"I believe the word you're looking for is horrible."

"That too. I don't see any tracks, but let's take a closer look just to make sure."

They inched closer. Joran studied the floor for any sign that someone had been here and found none. He wanted to scream his frustration, but that wouldn't help anything.

Mia stopped ten paces from the puddle of black ooze covering the floor. Even with the covering over their mouths, the stench burned Joran's nostrils.

"The dirt is smooth," Mia said. "No one's been here."

A vibration running through the floor provided their only warning before the pair of them went crashing into the darkness.

CHAPTER 24

Afull day in the sunken forest really amounted to about ten hours of usable light. In that time, Antius and the trackers covered maybe a third of the ground and found nothing save disappointment. Through the day's search, the trackers stayed far calmer than Antius felt. Every hour they spent wandering around down here let Bellator get further away. The renegade White Knight might be anywhere by the time they escaped his trap. Then they'd have to start their search from scratch with no real clues to follow.

As the shadows grew long, Trupo raised a hand. "Let's camp here for the night."

"Here" was a clearing surrounded by towering oaks that had just begun to turn orange. Under different circumstances, it would have made a nice spot for a picnic. Even the chirping birds sounded happy.

Helena and Cartus shrugged out of their packs and got busy setting up camp. With the bald giant now dead, Antius wondered who'd cook. He certainly had no talent for it. When traveling alone he usually just gnawed on preserved food as he went.

He went over to Trupo who had taken off his own pack and begun rummaging around for something. "We learned little enough today. Do you have any plans that might accelerate our search tomorrow?"

"No. And we did learn a great deal today. We learned where the exit isn't. In this line of work, patience is the most important thing. We may need a few days, but once we finish exploring the sinkhole, we will find our way out, assuming one exists. Then it's simply a matter of picking up Bellator's trail and running him down. Lucky for us, our best tracker survived. If she had to, Helena could track a hawk on the wind. So be at ease, we will complete the pope's task. You may depend on it."

Trupo's confidence soothed some of Antius's worry. Not all by any means, but some. With nothing useful to do, he found a spot at the base of an oak tree and settled down, wincing as he did. His ribs still ached from the impact with the tree branch. He felt pretty certain they were only bruised, but they still hurt.

Soon enough Trupo himself started a fire and set a stew pot to cooking. Fifteen minutes later the scent of simmering meat and vegetables filled the air. The trackers carried sealed packets filled with dried vegetables and herbs they mixed with water and meat. He'd never seen them before, but found the idea a good one.

Antius's mouth watered. He'd eaten nothing save two strips of jerky since they started the search. A hot meal would do wonders for him. Not as much as a cure all, but of course no alchemists made their home in the sinkhole.

Not that he could've afforded one in any case. Being a White Knight didn't come with a salary. Everything he had, the church provided.

An hour of simmering seemed to satisfy Trupo and he started dishing up bowls of soup. The sun had fully sunk behind the rim of the pit and the only light came from their fire. When Antius tried to take his bowl, Trupo didn't let go. The chief tracker had his head cocked as if listening to something Antius didn't hear.

"What?" Antius asked.

"The forest has gone silent. Something's out there."

Antius scrambled back and drew his sword.

A growl from the dark confirmed Trupo's guess. Another growl came from the opposite side. Two at least, probably more.

The trackers had their weapons out now and the group stood in a circle, back-to-back. Antius had no idea which direction he faced, but if the beasts showed themselves, he'd give them a taste of imperial steel. He had too much to do to die here.

A dark form, four-legged and low to the ground darted past at the edge of the light. Not a wolf or panther. Antius had never seen anything quite like the creature.

"They're toying with us," Helena said, her twin shortswords at the ready.

"That implies intelligence," Antius said. "You think these things are sentient?"

"I've seen weirder things in the provinces."

"Shut up and focus," Trupo said in a tense whisper.

An instant later one of the creatures leapt at Antius. He caught a glimpse of claws and fangs before he swung his sword with all his might.

The blow sent the beast flying. It whimpered and scurried back into the darkness.

It should have been chopped in half to lie twitching at his feet. A glance at his sword revealed a thin streak of blood. He'd cut it, but not deeply.

"Be careful," Antius said. "They're resistant to imperial steel."

"Any more good news?" Trupo asked.

No one answered.

From the darkness, three of the creatures emerged. They slunk closer and Antius finally had a chance to take a good look at them. He still had no idea what they were. Dark brown, almost black fur covered long, lithe bodies. Short legs kept them close to the ground while long snouts twitched as they sniffed.

"They look like oversized weasels," Cartus said.

It finally clicked for Antius. That's exactly what they looked like. But who ever heard of a weasel the size of a mastiff with fur tougher than imperial steel?

"Any suggestions?" Helena asked.

"Go for the eyes and mouth," Trupo said. "No fur to protect them."

Good thinking, but those were awfully small targets.

The weasels hissed and charged.

One of them rushed at Antius.

Three feet from him it opened its mouth, revealing needle-sharp three-inch fangs.

He thrust at its open mouth, hoping to score a quick kill.

Instead, the beast snapped down on his sword and tried to yank it out of his hand. Had they understood Trupo's plan? He didn't like to think so, but reality made it hard to doubt.

He played tug of war with the weasel, yanking with all his might. It felt like trying to free his weapon from a vise.

Antius braced himself and pulled hard.

The weasel let go, sending him stumbling back, staggering and fighting to stay on his feet. His opponent surged forward, eager to take advantage of the opening.

Five feet from him, Helena leapt, driving a shortsword into its back with all her weight behind the hit.

The weasel screeched and thrashed, trying to throw her off.

The female tracker bared her teeth and pushed harder, driving her sword deeper into its flesh.

Antius finally got himself under control and rushed forward in time to smash a second weasel aside as it leapt at Helena's unprotected back. His blow had little force behind it, but he did drive the creature back.

She joined him a moment later, bloody swords ready. "Thanks."

"Let's call it even." Antius turned, ready for the next round.

The weasel he hit had fled the field. Trupo and Cartus both looked okay. Between them lay the carcass of a second weasel.

Two dead monsters and no wounded on their side. A good result. He made a circle over his heart. The One God had been watching out for them.

"Everyone okay?" Trupo asked.

They all indicated they were.

"Don't know what those things are," Trupo said. "But I don't fancy them coming back for another visit while three of us are sleeping. We're going to have to rethink our watch schedule tonight. But first let's get those bodies out of here."

With Antius, Helena, and Trupo protecting him, Cartus dragged first one then the other giant weasel out of their camp and into the dark forest. That done, they salvaged as much soup as possible and ate.

In the end they decided one would sleep while the others kept watch. Antius's went first and managed a fitful three hours before Trupo shook him awake. If their search continued like this, exhaustion would render them easy prey for the monsters in short order.

Antius hated to think about those fangs sinking into him once he grew too tired to raise his sword.

———

After the single tensest night of his life, Antius was more than ready to get moving when the sun finally peeked over the lip of the sinkhole. From the trackers' tired, haggard faces, he suspected they felt the same. Breakfast amounted to jerky, biscuits, and dried fruit washed down by tepid water. He barely tasted it and soon enough they were on the move.

Helena took point today. She followed a faint blood trail left by one of the wounded weasels. Since they'd seen nothing big enough to make a meal for one of the beasts, much less four, Trupo said they must have a way out of the sinkhole. If a giant weasel could fit through it, a man would as well. Or so they hoped.

"Do you think they're nocturnal?" Antius asked.

Trupo shook his head. "No idea. Most likely they're holed up licking their wounds. By The One God, I've never hit anything as tough as their fur. You?"

"No, I can't say that I have. Imperial steel is supposed to be the sharpest, hardest substance in the world. Makes you wonder what their fur has in it."

Trupo grunted and turned his attention forward. That suited Antius fine as he had a lot to think about. He'd said he never hit anything as tough as the weasels' fur, and he hadn't, but he had seen something else that resisted imperial steel. Another giant beast that shouldn't exist: the black serpent. The legionnaires' weapons had bounced off that thing's scales like rain off a granite table. Giant weasels and giant serpents, it seemed impossible to Antius that the two weren't related, especially given Bellator's involvement with both.

Noon came and went with no sign that the weasels were slowing down or that they'd gained on them. They ate as they walked, no one wanting to take the time to make a fire lest it draw the attention of some other nasty thing lurking in the forest. Not that they'd seen anything. The birds seemed happy as they chirped, which eased Antius's worries a fraction.

An hour later Trupo pointed at the cliff wall ahead of them. "That must be their destination. Probably a tunnel or something."

Antius looked back the way they'd come. He wasn't a great tracker by any means, but a bit of dead reckoning made him think they were almost directly across from where they descended. Probably just a coincidence.

Midafternoon saw them at the foot of the cliff. Instead of a cave in the side of the cliff, the four of them stood around a set of stone stairs that led directly into the earth. The blood trail descended the stairs before vanishing into the darkness.

"Not at all what I expected," Trupo said. "Still, we don't have so many choices before us."

He took his pack off and pulled out a vial that glowed blue when he shook it.

"I didn't know you were an alchemist as well," Antius said.

Trupo chuckled. "I'm not. You can buy these things for a few gold pieces in any Second Circle alchemist's shop. I always keep a couple in my pack just in case we need to operate after sunset. Not the best way to fight, but certainly better than stumbling around in the dark."

Antius couldn't argue with that. No one else wanted to either and the group set out with Helena in the lead followed by Trupo with the light, then Antius, and finally Cartus bringing up the rear. The stairs allowed them to walk two by two, but they stayed single file anyway.

Forty-eight steps ended at a smooth stone passage that ran left to right for as far as the light revealed in either direction. The blood trail went right, but now that they'd found a passage, Antius wasn't sure they wanted to keep following the savage beasts. Avoiding a fight might be the smart move.

"Which way?" Helena asked.

"Stay on their trail," Trupo said.

"Wouldn't it be better to avoid the monsters?" Antius asked.

"Sure, but we have no idea what awaits us down the left branch. At least the weasels are hurt. That gives us an advantage, no matter how slight. The other way we might find something fully rested and uninjured."

"Or we might find the path clear," Antius said.

Trupo shrugged. "You want to go that way, be my guest. We're going right."

Since he had no desire to go off by himself, that ended the discussion.

As they walked Antius kept glancing at the walls of the tunnel. They appeared manmade and almost perfectly smooth. He'd never seen anything like them. No army of slaves armed with pickaxes and shovels made this passage. Neither did some digging monster. In truth, he hadn't the slightest idea what might have the power to create something like this and that fact worried him no end.

"There's a light up ahead," Helena said.

Her voice snapped Antius out of his daydream. Trupo put the light vial away and as soon as his eyes adjusted, Antius spotted the warm, yellow glow. He'd seen that shade of light before, it was the most common color used in alchemy jars. How one got down here he had no idea. It seemed he'd been thinking that a lot lately.

Everyone drew their weapons and Trupo said, "Let's go."

They slunk ahead, trying to keep quiet on the hard stone. The trackers did a far better job of it than Antius. He felt like a clumsy child compared to them.

Soon enough they reached an arched opening in the tunnel.

"Please come in," a voice from beyond the archway said. Antius would have sworn it came from a boy, but the idea of finding a child down here beggared the imagination. "I'm curious to see what sort of intruders are strong enough to kill two of my pets."

The group shared nervous looks, but unless they turned around, they had no choice but to obey the request.

They had no discussion, Trupo simply strode through the opening and the rest of them followed. In a high-backed chair that served as the room's sole piece of furniture sat a hooded figure, the two wounded weasels at his side. The size looked about right for a boy, but seated, Antius couldn't say for sure. He wore a mottled brown cloak, matching tunic and trousers, and black leather boots, one of which rested on the seat of his chair, putting his right knee near his chest.

As for the light, it seemed to have no source, instead filling the entire empty chamber with a diffused glow.

"Ah, another White Knight, I should have known. You people are certainly tough. Though you're in better shape than the last one my pets dragged back here. He was nearly dead."

"Bellator," Antius said. "What did you do to twist his mind?"

"Do? I healed him and introduced him to the archbishop. After the church killed his soulmate, we had no need to try and recruit him. He offered to help us so fast it would have made your head spin. Usually when someone loses their soulmate, they end up committing suicide." The hooded man scratched his chin. "Though I suppose an overwhelming desire for revenge isn't that uncommon either when murder is involved."

"His soulmate?" Antius's mind reeled. Bellator must have met him or her on his pilgrimage. Surely a sign that The One God favored his mission. "Who did that?"

"How should I know?" The more Antius heard the more certain he felt that they dealt with a child not yet in his teens. "Bellator never said beyond 'dogs of the church.' I had no idea the church used hunting dogs. Ever since he mentioned them, I've wanted to get my hands on one. I bet I could turn it into something amazing. Anyway, are you lot here to join up?"

"We're looking for the way back to the surface," Trupo said. "We have pressing business above."

"That's too bad. The archbishop said anyone that finds this place either has to join The One True God cult or, well, I'm sure you can guess." The boy touched the arm of his chair.

A tremor ran through the floor and the next thing Antius knew, he found himself falling straight down a shaft into The One God alone knew what danger.

CHAPTER 25

Somehow Joran kept his grip on the light vial as he and Mia rolled down a ramp into some huge cavern he didn't even know existed under Fort Death's basement. Mia sprang instantly to her feet, sword raised and ready. For his part, Joran got up a good deal more slowly. Every bit of him hurt from that little tumble. That said, at least nothing felt broken.

He held the light above his head and looked all around. The cavern stretched as far as the light reached in every direction. Massive columns of stone supported the ceiling. What interested Joran more than anything was the tube running from a pool of Black Bile ten feet across and he didn't want to imagine how deep up through the ceiling. The bile spring appeared to be manmade. He'd never imagined such a possibility and seriously doubted anyone else in the empire had either.

Of course, that begged the question, were the other bile springs around the world manmade as well?

He had no idea where to find them much less how to determine their origin.

Movement at the edge of his light caught Joran's attention.

Something shuffled toward them. First one, then three, then ten, all of them men dressed in crimson imperial uniforms. They all had slightly melted features and onyx black eyes. They looked like the corrupted woman Joran and Mia fought in Tiber only even less aware.

"One mystery solved," Joran muttered.

"What a surprise," a cold, deep voice said. "My assassin failed to kill you and now here you are, delivering yourself up for execution. This must be my lucky day."

"Run!" Mia said.

"I think not," the voice countered.

The ramp creaked as it started to rise.

Joran spun and hurled the adhesive vial. It shattered, sticking the ramp to the floor. The glue stretched a foot before hardening and locking the passage open.

He sprinted toward the ramp, Mia a step behind.

"No!" the voice shouted. "Kill them all!"

The thud of pursuing feet hastened their steps.

As soon as they hit the basement, Joran pulled another vial, this one filled with alchemist's fire. Maybe the guards were too afraid to use it in the city, but he didn't care if he burned the whole damn fort to the ground. Maybe that would bury that cursed cavern and whoever lived down there along with the still-moving remains of the dead soldiers.

Flames exploded when the vial crashed into the ramp. He saw dozens of black-eyed corpses shuffling around down there. They backed away from the fire, but it didn't seem to overly worry them, assuming they were capable of worry.

"You've done enough," Mia said. "Let's get out of here. We'll need the army to deal with this."

"If those things are as tough as the one we fought, the army won't have a chance. At least I didn't see any more of those black swords."

They hurried out of the basement and up the stairs to where Caeso and the rest of the team waited.

"Is all well, my lord?" Caeso asked.

"Not in the least," Joran said. "We're leaving, now."

Bless him, he didn't ask another question, instead falling in behind Mia and Joran in their mad dash to the keep exit. They ran until they reached the man left behind to tend the horses. They all mounted up, but Joran didn't ride at once for Tiber. He expected flames to come roaring out of the keep as the alchemist's fire spread.

A minute passed and then two and still no flames. Those things must have extinguished them, but Joran failed to imagine how. Even water wouldn't douse alchemist's fire once it got going. Doubtless some other magic he didn't understand was responsible.

"We need to keep people well away from the fort," Joran said. "The last thing we need is for those things to capture some farmers or other travelers and use them to increase their numbers. Any ideas?"

"The main southern trade road runs only a few miles from here," Caeso said. "This time of year, hundreds if not thousands of merchants and their guards travel north to trade in Tiber. There's no way we can turn them all back."

"No more talk," Mia said. "Those things have reached the courtyard. We'll have to hope for the best until we can let Her Majesty know what's happening."

Joran hated it, but Mia was right. He urged his horse into motion. Three days back plus however long they'd need to muster a legion or two. He shook his head. The One God alone knew what might happen between now and then.

———

Overseer stared in disbelief as the two mortals fled up the stuck-open ramp. He'd had them and still they escaped his trap. It seemed impossible that the man should always have the exact thing he needed in his hand. He'd assumed his agents' incompetence had allowed Joran Den Cade to get the best of them, but now he wondered if the young nobleman didn't have the luck of a demon on his side.

"Kill them!" he shouted at his bile zombies.

Scores of undead shuffled forward.

They'd barely reached the base of the ramp when flames exploded in front of them. Alchemist's fire, naturally the whelp would have some of that on him.

At his mental command the bile zombies stopped. The flames wouldn't kill them, but they would degrade their bodies and possibly render them useless. Unlike Lovia, these crude creations lacked her powerful healing abilities. They also lacked her fragment of awareness. Though her mind deteriorated quickly, she retained enough will to act on a simple order without his constant attention.

Unfortunately, it took days to create a single zombie with her characteristics and he had other things to focus on.

Snarling away his annoyance, Overseer focused on the ether and commanded it to suppress the fire. Half a minute later he'd snuffed it out and another command sent his servants up and after the fleeing humans.

Though slow and stupid, the zombies were relentless. They'd pursue Joran and the girl until they were destroyed or their prey dead.

He left them to their work, stood, and strode over to the bile spring. He breathed deeply, savoring the corruption and power radiating from the Black Bile. When his body fairly crackled with dark energy, he focused on the archbishop.

The mirror-smooth surface of the pool shimmered and the

archbishop's pale, beautiful face appeared. Black lips peeled back from perfect white teeth. Elongated eyeteeth and eyes as red as rubies made it clear that she was as far from human as Overseer himself.

"Trouble?" she asked.

"How did you know?" Overseer asked. Surely she hadn't read his mind from so far away.

"You're not due to update me until next week. And I know you don't enjoy our conversations so much that you contact me without a good reason. What has happened?"

"The cavern has been discovered. The Den Cade whelp again."

The archbishop cocked her head. "Last time we spoke, you assured me your assassin would deal with him. What happened?"

"Turns out a cure all will neutralize the bile and kill even an advanced bile zombie. I hadn't expected that. Somehow they bound Lovia and forced a cure all into her chest cavity."

"And the sword I provided for your champion?"

"Seized by the brat," Overseer said through clenched teeth.

"Disappointing. Hell-forged black iron swords aren't so easy to come by after all. What is your plan to recover it?"

"I don't know for sure, but I assume it's in the palace in Tiber. All our agents in the palace have been exposed and either been captured or fled. I have no more cells in Tiber to call on."

"So you have no plan." Her displeasure hit him like a slap to the face. "It seems I shall have to dispatch someone to clean up your mess."

Overseer lowered his head. "Thank you, Archbishop. But the reason I contacted you—"

"Yes, I didn't forget. The cavern has been compromised and you want to know what to do. Well, there's nothing we can do about your most recent failure now. Losing our hidden base so close to Tiber is a blow, but hardly a mortal one. Send your bile zombies out to do as much damage as possible, erase the rune circle, and return to base."

"As you command. What about my other cells throughout the empire?"

"You may continue to run them for the time being. Annoyed as I am with you, we knew someone in the empire might eventually smoke us out. The attempt on the emperor was worth the risk. Pity it failed, but even we can't expect to win all the time."

"Understood, Archbishop. I will return shortly."

Her face vanished, leaving the pool dark and empty once more. He'd survived the conversation and even retained his rank as an overseer, a far better result than he'd feared. Still, best to hurry and carry out her commands. One more failure might be enough to tip the scales against him.

And if that happened, no power in the world would save Overseer from the archbishop's wrath.

CHAPTER 26

The dark shaft spit Antius out none too gently into an open space surrounded by broken buildings. The rest of the trackers dropped from the square opening and he rolled aside in time to narrowly avoid acting as a cushion for them. He didn't even have a chance to stand before the square shaft retracted up into the ceiling until the opening was flush with the stone about thirty feet above them. No way were they escaping that way.

He finally stood and looked around. They'd ended up in a park filled with long-dead, dried-up grass. More broken buildings of various heights jutted up in the distance. It looked like they'd ended up in an underground ruined city. An unnerving purplish light filled the cavern, just bright enough to let them see, but still dark enough to hide the details. Though it failed to hide the musty, slightly rotten odor that filled the air.

"Where are we now?" Trupo glared around at the city as if expecting it to provide an answer.

To Antius's surprise, the voice from the boy upstairs said, "You're in the maze. No, it's not a real maze, the archbishop wouldn't let me build one, but it does come close. My pets like to hunt the rats that live down there. But they're not fussy, meat is meat after all. Have fun."

"Wait!" Antius said. "Is this some kind of test? Are we supposed to find the exit or something?"

"I suppose it is a test," the voice said. "But not for you. Killing humans is good practice for my pets. Since you beat two of them in the forest, I guess they need more training."

"What about the exit?" Antius asked.

"What exit? No one leaves the maze except in the belly of my beasts."

Antius and the trackers shared looks. That hadn't sounded good at all. Still, if the weasels had a way of getting into the city, surely they could use the same passage to escape.

"We need to find a defensive position before something hungry shows up," Trupo said. "Helena, take point. If you see any fresh tracks, steer us the other way."

The female tracker set out and the rest of them fell in behind her. Their footfalls, even the trackers', sounded incredibly loud in the silence as they echoed around the gigantic cavern.

After a hundred yards Antius had to ask. "Did you kill Bellator's soulmate on the pope's orders?"

"Let's focus on getting out of here in one piece," Trupo said.

"I have to know."

"No. When His Holiness dispatched us, no one said anything about Bellator even having a soulmate."

"And Bellator himself?" Antius pressed.

"The pope told us that despite his best efforts to discourage Bellator's quest, the White Knight refused to be dissuaded. The Prophet's path had to be taken on faith, he said. By trying to prove the truth of it, Bellator had lost his faith and thus no longer had the standing to be a White Knight. We were told to stop him, one way or another. The woman we found at his camp attacked us, so we defended ourselves. After a brief chase, Bellator leapt from the cliff where we descended. We assumed he died on impact, but obviously we were wrong."

"Bellator had the strongest faith of any White Knight I ever served with. Since the pope is no fool, he had to know that."

Trupo shrugged. "We work for the church. His Holiness is very generous with our compensation, so when he tells me to do something, I don't ask a ton of questions. One White Knight more or less is hardly the end of the world."

Antius bristled at the implied threat.

"Shhh!" Helena said. "Something's coming."

Everyone drew their weapons and formed a defensive circle.

"Where?" Trupo asked.

"Not sure. Everything echoes in here. I heard scurrying ahead of us, I think, but I saw nothing."

"Maybe the rats our host mentioned?" Antius said.

That turned out to be wishful thinking on his part. A creature far bigger than the weasels they'd fought lumbered out of the shadows. It stood nearly seven feet tall at the shoulder, thick, no doubt sword-resistant hair hung from a barrel-like body and covered its thick legs. The creature's head vaguely resembled a bear if you smushed its muzzle flat into its face. Two tusks like a boar's jutted from its lower jaw.

"What, by The One God, is that?" Antius asked.

The beast decided to answer for itself, loosing a roar that shook the cavern. It stomped one foot hard enough to crack the stone floor.

They got no more warning before it charged.

Antius dove right, avoiding getting crushed by inches.

He rolled to his feet, and slashed at the passing hind quarter. His sword hit the heavy fur and bounced off without making a mark. The creature didn't so much as flinch.

Twenty yards away it started to turn for a second pass.

Antius risked a glance at his companions and let out a breath of relief to find them all alive and intact. Little as he cared for mercenaries that killed for coin, even the church's coin, he had a better chance of escaping this death trap with their help than he did on his own.

"Any ideas?" Antius asked. "My sword didn't even scratch that thing."

The monster had nearly completed its turn when Trupo said, "Let's put some buildings between us. Maybe if it loses sight of us, it'll get bored and wander off."

That seemed overly optimistic to Antius, but he didn't have a better idea, so when the mercenaries ran, he followed.

They dodged down a narrow alley, across another street, and ran right through a barely standing pile of rubble. Finally, Trupo stopped behind an intact stone wall. He bent over and gasped for breath. Antius pressed his back against the stone and tried to calm his racing heart. He'd spent far too much time fleeing from giant monsters lately.

A faint vibration ran through his spine. He jumped left a moment before the wall exploded and the creature came charging through.

Helena got less lucky. A tusk caught her in the side and a toss of the beast's head sent her flying.

Antius charged, sword pointed like a spear. If slashing wouldn't work, maybe this would.

The tip hit and dug in.

The beast roared and when it did Trupo leapt, shoving his blade into the underside of its mouth and up into its brain.

The creature collapsed, twitched a few times, and went still.

Trupo and Cartus ignored the dead monster and ran over to Helena. The pair knelt beside their fallen comrade. Antius kept watch while they tended to her. He seriously doubted that thing lived alone down here.

"Hang on, Helena," Trupo said. "We'll get you patched up."

Antius took a quick glance over his shoulder. The size of the hole in Helena's abdomen told him everything he needed to know about her situation. If she had five more minutes, he'd be shocked.

"Wow!" the familiar and now-hated voice from above said. "You killed my cruncher and only lost one of your team. That's amazing. It also tells me I need to find some way to protect the inside of my pets' mouths. Thank you for that."

"You son of bitch!" Trupo roared as he stood. "When I get my hands on you I'm going to wring your neck!"

"Were you not paying attention earlier?" the voice said, sounding genuinely confused. "You're not going to get your hands on me. You're going to be eaten by my pets. The cruncher was the slowest and stupidest of the bunch down there. But don't worry, the noise of your fight will have drawn the attention of something more interesting. Try to make it a good show."

"I could easily get to hate him," Trupo said.

"Helena?"

"Gone. That thing's tusk tore her liver and punctured a lung. She didn't have a chance."

Antius made a circle over his heart. "May she rest easy in The One God's embrace."

"So say we all," Trupo and Cartus said in unison to Antius's considerable surprise. Perhaps their faith wasn't just for show after all.

"What now?" Cartus asked.

"Our situation hasn't really changed," Trupo said. "We still need to find a way out of here or, failing that, somewhere safe to hole up. I say we pick the sturdiest-looking building, make it as defensible as possible, and see what shows up. Once we have an idea what we're dealing with down here, we can look for the exit."

"And if that freak upstairs was telling the truth and there is no exit?" Cartus asked.

Trupo shrugged. "Then we take as many of his monsters with us as we can."

The mercenary's grim tone mirrored Antius's thoughts. He had to find a way out of here, had to know what Bellator learned that convinced the pope he needed to die. Antius had never been so certain of anything in his life.

Whatever Bellator learned would change his life, and maybe the world, forever.

———

Beastmaster hopped off his throne. He thought of the chair in his meeting chamber as a throne, though some would claim that since he only ruled over beasts, he wasn't much of a king. Not that anyone had ever said that to him. If they had, he'd have fed them to his pets.

The new arrivals were doing better than he'd hoped. Maybe they'd provide some entertainment for a week or two. It got so boring here sometimes. The archbishop said his work was important and he did enjoy finding new ways to improve his pets, but he so seldom got a chance to really test them. That's why he sent a psychic command to the beasts of the maze to leave them alone until he returned. He had to report their arrival to her before he could play any more.

One of the giant weasels rubbed her nose against his hip hoping for a pat. Her wounds had already closed and he sensed no pain when he reached out and touched her thoughts.

"Good girl." He patted her head and stroked her back.

She purred as he pet her. Her mate forced his way over, wanting his share of attention. Soon enough he had them both purring. Weasels didn't normally do that, but he'd altered their vocal cords to give them the ability. Not that it made them any stronger, he just thought it sounded cute.

"That's enough, you two," Beastmaster said. "I have to talk to the archbishop now."

They both shied away when he mentioned the group's leader. The weasels had met her when she last checked in on his work and neither of them liked her. Something about her scent made them uncomfortable. The fact that she was technically dead probably didn't help either.

He left his current favorites behind and skipped down the hall to his scrying chamber. Beastmaster preferred to look through the eyes of his pets, but that didn't allow for conversation. His talents were mainly focused on transmuting and altering living creatures, but he had enough general skill to use a crystal ball.

At the end of the hall, he stopped in front of a blank wall. Placing his hand on the rough surface, he focused on the ether and sent a stream of it into the stone. A section of wall dropped out of sight and he stepped through. The scrying chamber held only a low table with a head-sized crystal ball resting on a silver tripod.

Beastmaster placed his fingers on the smooth, cool crystal and projected his awareness into it. Next, he imagined the archbishop. A few seconds later it felt like a pair of giant hands grabbed his psychic body and dragged him across space. In an instant he found himself standing in a dark chamber facing the pale figure of the cult's leader. She wore an elaborate black leather dress with strategic cutouts that revealed patches of fish-belly-white skin.

To Beastmaster's surprise, she wasn't alone. One of the overseers, he never could tell them apart, especially in the psychic realm, stood right at the edge of his perception like a humanoid blob of corrupt ether.

"This certainly is my day for chats. Beastmaster, I trust all's well."

"Very well. I got some new playmates for my pets. A White

Knight and three mercenaries. I guess two mercenaries now since one of them died in the maze. They're pretty tough, even killed a cruncher."

"How did they end up in the sunken forest?" the archbishop asked.

Beastmaster cocked his head. "I didn't think to ask. From what I overheard, the pope sent them to hunt down Bellator. Not sure why they thought he'd still be at my place."

"Probably because that's the last place they saw him. My agents spotted the group heading that way and I warned Samaritan."

"How come I didn't get a warning?" Beastmaster asked.

"Because you didn't need one. Your pets would have sensed them as soon as they arrived and while I suspected they might end up in the forest, I deemed it equally possible Samaritan might have found some way to deal with them before they arrived. I would've hated to get your hopes up only to dash them."

"That's fair, I guess. Did you want me to do anything in particular with them or is it okay to let my pets eat them?"

"I have no use for them. The White Knight probably knows little that Samaritan didn't already tell me and the mercenaries are of even less value."

"Okay. Any new orders for me?"

"No, but as long as you're here, how do the experiments progress?"

"I'm kind of stuck. Once I increase any animal's size beyond about four times their natural maximum, I have to use so much Black Bile that they become berserk and uncontrollable. I've been focusing on giving them other abilities instead."

"It seems we must have missed something in the process." The archbishop's beautiful face twisted in a frown. "If only we could find the ancient capital…"

"That's outside my area of expertise," Beastmaster said. "Can I go now?"

A moment later his psychic self slammed into his physical self hard enough to make his head ache and spots dance before his eyes. She always got so cranky when she talked about that place. Such obsession had to be bad for you. Not that he was so much better. His obsessions simply ran down a different track.

Shaking his head to clear the spots, he jogged out of the scrying chamber and back to his throne room. Time to see how his guests handled his next pet.

CHAPTER 27

Two and a half days of hard riding saw Joran and his companions back on the palace grounds. They'd arrived in the early afternoon and Joran felt as sore and tired as he ever had. Only adrenaline and the knowledge of what lurked under Fort Death kept him upright and moving.

He and Mia left the investigation team to take the horses to the stable and hurried into the palace. They needed to find Alexandra or her brother. Joran didn't dream he'd be able to simply walk in and talk to the emperor himself, despite being engaged to his daughter.

They went right to the suite they shared with Alexandra. Joran didn't bother to knock. As soon as he entered, a pair of beautiful servants hurried into the sitting room from their chamber in the back. If they were resting there, it meant Alexandra had gone out.

Naturally, when he really needed to talk to her, she would be somewhere else.

"Lord Den Cade," the nearest servant said. "How may we be of service?"

"Where's Alexandra?"

"In court, with her father and brother. They should be finishing up in a couple hours if you'd like to wait."

Joran shook his head. Every minute counted.

"I'm afraid I can't. Thank you for your help."

She curtsied and they left the suite.

"Is it me or does our luck seem to stink lately?" Mia asked.

"On the contrary, since we're still alive after everything that's happened, I'd say our luck is extraordinarily good."

He led the way through the halls, nodding absently to servants and guards as they passed, but never slowing. At last they stood outside the doors to the throne room. Two imperial guards stood impassively on either side of them.

"Court's closed, my lord," the guard on the right said.

Joran held up his amulet and said, "It's an emergency. I'll take full responsibility, but you have to let me in right now."

The guards looked at his amulet then at each other, clearly debating which decision would get them in less trouble. After what seemed far too long, but was probably only a minute, the guard that spoke nodded and they opened the right-hand door just enough for Mia and Joran to slip inside.

Scores of nobles filled the space. At the front, the emperor sat on the eagle throne flanked by Alexandra and her brother. A skinny noble in a fur-trimmed robe stood before them and droned on about something to do with water rights. It hardly seemed important enough for the emperor himself to address, but since he'd missed all the context, Joran couldn't say for sure.

Alexandra had worn her finest crimson and silver robes. She was trying to pay attention, but Joran had spent enough time with her at this point to recognize her boredom. Her gaze drifted around the room and her eyes widened when they settled on him.

Joran made a fist, held up his index finger, and spun it to the right. He'd seen the Iron Guards use that sign and felt pretty confident that it meant "emergency."

Alexandra nodded and leaned down to whisper in her father's ear.

The emperor raised a hand, silencing the nobleman midsentence. "A matter has come to our attention. Court is closed for the day and will resume here next session. You are all dismissed."

A few people grumbled, but most rose from their uncomfortable benches, bowed to the throne, and filed out the now-open doors. How the guards knew to open them, Joran had no idea. Maybe they heard the emperor speak.

He shoved aside the irrelevant thought and strode up to the throne. When the doors had clunked shut he said, "We have a problem. Fort Death has fallen and the soldiers have been transformed into creatures like the one that killed so many people in First Circle. I don't know what a full garrison is, but I'm guessing at least three score."

"The One God be merciful," Alexandra said. "It's more like ten score and all of them like that creature you killed? There isn't enough cure all in the empire to destroy that many."

"Why don't you tell us everything that happened, son," the emperor said.

Joran did so as quickly and succinctly as possible. "We had no hope of stopping them with the forces available, so we rode back at best speed. The creatures do seem at least hesitant when confronted by fire and they looked less aware than the one in the city. I think alchemist's fire may work on these, but the sooner we deal with them, the better."

"What do you mean, less aware?" Marcus asked.

"The one in First Circle seemed to have a purpose, a goal. This bunch just lurched around at whoever controlled them's command. They seemed slower and mindless."

The emperor stood. "Whatever they are, I can't very well have a couple hundred of them roaming the area around Tiber. Muster out the Second Legion. Four thousand men should be enough to hunt them down. Joran, you and Mia will advise General Artum."

"I can take command, Father," Alexandra said.

"Too dangerous, at least until we better understand what we're dealing with. I want you to organize the scribes and find out exactly how many people served at that fort. Every one of them needs to be accounted for. Marcus, you'll coordinate the city defenses. If, The One God forbid, these things reach Tiber, I want a plan in place to stop them."

Alexandra's face twisted a fraction, but she nodded. "Yes, Father. Do you wish me to give the order to muster the Second before I get started?"

"Good idea. You can introduce Joran to General Artum. That should smooth things over considerably." The emperor clapped once. "These lunatics have brought the battle to our homeland. Let's show them what happens to those that dare challenge the empire."

They all bowed and Joran, Mia, and Alexandra hurried out of the throne room. When they'd put some distance between them and the emperor Alexandra snarled. "Too dangerous? I'm the supreme commander of the army. Handling dangerous things is my job!"

"This is far too small-scale to require the Iron Princess's personal involvement," Joran said. "You nearly got killed a couple times lately, maybe your father is nervous for you."

"Ha! If he plans to keep me locked up in the palace, I'm going to go nuts. I wanted to murder those prattling idiots five minutes after they started talking." She seemed to be in full Iron Princess mode today.

Alexandra pushed through a palace door and marched outside into the courtyard. The sprawling barracks that housed the First and Second legions sat a quarter mile from the palace proper. Joran had never visited the barracks, but doubted they were anything too interesting.

Halfway between the palace and the barracks Alexandra stopped and turned to face him. "I may not really be the Iron Princess, but she needs to exist and if Father coddles me too much, the illusion will break. And once it does, there will be no putting it back together."

"Would that be such a bad thing?" he asked. "No more pretending, no danger. You'd be free to be yourself."

"I'd also have no authority and nothing to do beyond princess stuff in the palace. I love Marcus's wife like she's my own sister, but if I had to sit around sewing and watching the kids with her, I'd burn the palace down inside of a week. Besides, I'm damn good at leading the army, even if I do have to adopt a persona to do it."

"Then I don't know what to tell you," Joran said. "The emperor certainly won't listen to anything I might say. I'm sure once a more conventional enemy appears, the Iron Princess will be back in action."

She offered a faint smile and hugged him. "Thanks."

The soldiers outside the barracks all snapped to attention when they spotted Alexandra approaching. One of the men, Joran put his age at thirtyish, with a gold, sword-shaped prefect's badge pinned to his tunic brought his fist to his heart. "How may we serve, Majesty?"

"The homeland is in danger, Prefect, and my father has decided the Second will eliminate the threat. Prepare your men and point me toward General Artum."

"General Artum has gone into the city, Majesty."

"Has he? Was the Second's status as the ready legion not made clear?" Alexandra took a step closer to the prefect. "You do know what it means to be the ready legion, do you not?"

"We are to be prepared to march day or night with ten minutes' notice, Majesty."

"Very good, Prefect. Now, for a more difficult question. How does the legion march without its general present?"

"I... I don't know, Majesty. Things have been so peaceful. General Artum saw no harm in spending the day in the city. What do you wish me to do?"

"Prepare the legion. I will assume command. When we return, I will discipline the general. And Prefect, you had best be lined up and ready to march in ten minutes or so help me I'll see the Second rotated out to the frontier to hunt bandits!" She practically screamed those last two words.

Joran actually felt bad for the prefect. He couldn't exactly order the general to do the right thing. Beside him Mia had a huge grin plastered on her face. She seemed to greatly enjoy Alexandra's Iron Princess routine.

Alexandra grabbed a convenient legionnaire. "Take a message to my brother. Tell him I was forced to assume command of the Second and he'll need to assign someone to handle the scribes. He'll know what needs to be done."

All the blood had drained from the young man's face. "No one will let me speak to the crown prince, Majesty."

"Just tell the imperial guards that I sent you. They can relay the message. Hurry. I expect you back here in time to march."

The soldier sprinted off.

"There, Father can't complain if I had to take over for an absent general." Alexandra looked down at her formal robe. "Not exactly ideal for going to war, but given the rush, it'll have to do. Now, tell me how to kill these creatures so I don't sound like a total idiot when I address the legion."

Joran had learned from his father how to pick his battles, especially where Mother was concerned. While he and Alexandra weren't married yet, he assumed the same principles applied.

"I'll tell you my theory about how to kill them. And remember, until we've actually succeeded, that's all this is."

"Equivocation noted. Now talk."

Mia giggled and Joran and Alexandra both turned to look at her.

"What?" Alexandra asked.

"Nothing, it's just you two already sound married." She cleared her throat and smoothed her expression. "Pretend I never said anything."

Alexandra muttered something Joran didn't catch and raised an eyebrow.

"Right. I figure we need to burn the bodies completely to ash. That's going to take alchemist's fire, and assuming the Black Bile makes them resistant, probably a lot. Out in the open that's no problem, but if we're not careful, we risk a forest fire at minimum and potentially damage to any settlements in the area."

"Not an issue," Alexandra said. "We need to stop these things no matter the cost. The empire will pay to repair any damage the legion causes. The real problem will be figuring out how many we've destroyed and how many remain. If any slip past, who knows what damage they might cause."

"Can't we just note their numbers and make certain it matches how many served in the garrison?" Mia asked.

"If we knew without a doubt that the enemy didn't trans-form any passing farmers or merchants, sure, but if they did, we might think we were done when there were still a dozen or more monsters wandering around out there."

"That may be a risk we have to accept," Joran said. "There's simply no way to know for sure how many of the things we're dealing with."

"I hate it, but you're right. Once we've dealt with the bulk of them, I'll order roving patrols through the forest and general area of the fort as well as increasing cavalry patrols along the southern trade road."

"We need to secure Fort Death as well," Joran said. "You can't imagine how much Black Bile is under there."

"Right, sounds like we have our plan of action. Time to address the legion."

Alexandra strode off, back straight and looking every bit the Iron Princess despite her flowing crimson and silver robes and lack of armor and weapons. Joran and Mia followed along behind her and he smiled. Palace life was definitely not for Alexandra.

Hopefully they'd all survive long enough to figure out where they truly belonged.

CHAPTER 28

Antius and the surviving mercenaries settled on a two-story square stone building that looked a bit like a castle lookout tower and even better had the same sturdy construction. The foot-thick walls should stand up even to a charge from one of those things—a cruncher, the madman upstairs called it—they'd fought earlier.

The first level consisted of a single room filled with rotten wood that once might have been furniture, but now looked suitable for mouse bedding at best. Cartus descended the steps at the rear of the room.

"How'd it look?" Trupo asked.

"Not great. There used to be a hatch allowing access to the roof. It's rotted down to nothing leaving a two-foot square hole in the ceiling. I don't know how we'll seal it up."

"We won't," Trupo said. "We'll leave the lower level empty and camp upstairs. The roof access and staircase will be easier to defend than the huge open doorway down here."

"Doesn't leave us a path for a quick getaway," Antius said.

Trupo offered a bitter laugh. "Where do you plan to escape to? It's a death trap in every direction."

"How are we fixed for water?" Cartus asked. "I haven't seen anything to drink down here, but if those beasts live here all the time, there must be a source."

"Ten days," Trupo said. "Maybe two weeks if we ration it. Don't worry, I doubt dying of thirst will be our fate."

Antius left the mercenaries to their discussion and climbed the stairs to the second floor. Trupo, at least, appeared to have lost his will to survive. From now on, Antius would make his own decisions and if the others wanted to follow him, so be it. He wouldn't be dragged down by Trupo's weakness.

The second floor looked much the same as the first save for the square hole in the ceiling. Defending that opening would be fairly easy, assuming they weren't also fighting something trying force its way up the stairs.

He walked over to a spot directly below the hole, leapt, and caught the edge in an iron grip. He chinned himself up and looked around at the roof. Perfectly flat with a three-foot wall to stop anyone from walking off of it. It almost looked like a place to hold a party. He could picture the well-dressed guests chatting while servants drifted about offering drinks and snacks.

Of course, that mental image assumed this place used to be on the surface. Having a party under a dark cavern ceiling held considerably less appeal than having it under the moon and stars.

A shadow flashed overhead.

Antius dropped an instant ahead of some winged thing that flew through the space he'd occupied a moment earlier. He caught only a glimpse of leathery wings then it was gone.

A bat maybe, albeit one the size of a swan. He shook his head. Doubtful it would be something as nice as a bat, much less a swan.

Something crashed on the first floor before he had a chance to shout a warning about the thing that nearly hit him.

He managed three steps before Trupo and Cartus came sprinting up the steps. They both spun at the top and faced a monster that resembled a bear with a mouth big enough to swallow a toddler whole. It had rows of teeth like a shark and snapped at Trupo's sword as if unafraid of getting stabbed.

"We could use a hand here," Cartus said.

"I'd be only too happy to oblige," Antius said, turning back to the opening in the ceiling. "Unfortunately, some flying thing nearly took my head off a minute ago and I'd just as soon avoid having it sneak up on us."

Roars and snarls mingled with grunts and thuds behind him, but Antius didn't take his eyes off the opening.

And a good thing too. A shifting shadow gave him his only warning. The beast he spotted earlier dove at the roof access.

Antius swung with all his might, meeting the creature head on as it entered.

His sword clashed against a foot-long snout as hard as imperial steel.

Vibrations ran up his hands as the bat thing flapped around the second floor, wobbly as a drunk after a bender. If the impact had nearly numbed Antius's hands, he couldn't imagine what it did to the monster's brain.

He drew back for another swing, hoping to finish it off before it recovered its wits.

A moment later a roar preceded something heavy slamming into him.

Antius staggered and fell, a limp weight across his legs and chest. Much as he didn't want to look, he turned his gaze upon the body.

It was Trupo, or what remained of him anyway. His chest had been caved in, the ribs broken and driven into his internal organs. An ugly but quick way to go.

He kicked the body off of him and scrambled to his feet just in time to fend off another dive bomb from the bat creature.

As it flew off to make another pass, he glanced at Cartus. The final mercenary had retreated enough to allow the bear creature to reach the top of the steps. If it got all the way into the second floor they were doomed.

They needed to find a new place to hide. He threw his sword up onto the roof, ran, leapt, grabbed the lip of the access hatch and pulled himself onto the roof. "Come on, Cartus!"

He reached back down to help the mercenary up. He might as well not have bothered. The bat thing had run him through the back of the neck, its nose sword, as Antius had come to think of it, jutting out the front.

Antius collected his sword, sheathed it, and hurried to the side of the tower. The nearest building was a long jump away and only one story tall. Not ideal, but given his options he refused to hesitate. With a running leap he kicked off the safety wall and fell ten feet to the next roof.

The moment his feet hit, he crashed through the rotten wood and landed in a heap below. Coughing and waving away the dust, he forced himself to sit up. Everything hurt, but nothing felt broken. Much like when he fell from the cliff face, it seemed he'd avoided serious injury.

But that wouldn't last if those monsters found him. Even worse, he didn't have anyone to help him fight the beasts off.

Alone and with nothing save his faith to aid him, Antius left the smashed building behind and ran as far and fast as possible away from the horrors that had killed his companions.

CHAPTER 29

Marching the entire Second Legion south to Fort Death took a fair bit longer than Joran had needed to ride back to the palace. The soldiers marched in neat rows, with scouts deployed well ahead. They also took up the entire road, so any merchants they met had to stop and pull off to the side to let them pass. Everyone did this quickly and without a word of complaint. Probably because they knew any complaints would fall on deaf ears at best and draw the ire of the Iron Princess at worst.

Ordinarily, Alexandra would have ridden at the head of the legion, but given the danger and the fact that they had no idea where or when they were likely to make contact, Joran had convinced her to ride in the center surrounded by her Iron Guards as well as four centuries of infantry. That he and Mia got to ride beside her with the same protection made a nice bonus.

"We should reach Fort Death tomorrow, Majesty." The unlucky prefect, Dantius, that greeted Alexandra upon her arrival to the Second Legion's barracks had been pressed into service as her aide de camp. The poor man looked in danger of fainting every time he had to update her, but he'd done a remarkable job of keeping his wits about him.

"Finally," Alexandra said. "The One God knows how far those blasted monsters have spread in a week."

A shout went up from the head of the column. "Scout approaching."

Alexandra and Joran shared a look. They still had half a day before setting up camp for the night. Only one thing would bring a scout back this early: enemy contact.

The neat rows of infantry parted to let the mounted scout through. His horse had been whipped to a lather and it panted almost as loudly as its rider.

"Majesty," the scout said. "We spotted one of the creatures you described about a mile ahead. The rest of my squad are keeping a discreet eye on it. It's made no aggressive moves, seeming content to shamble slowly along on the side of the road."

"Only one?" Alexandra muttered to herself. "I'd assumed whoever controlled these things would have them fight in groups."

"We may encounter groups later," Joran said, "But for a test of my basic theory, this is perfect."

"I suppose." Alexandra didn't sound the least bit certain. "Alright, take a century, and see if you can kill it, or destroy it, I guess, since it's already dead."

"First Century!" Dantius shouted. "Advance for special duty!"

A hundred men separated themselves from the legion and marched a little ways ahead before stopping to wait for Joran and Mia, who quickly dismounted and handed their reins to one of the Iron Guards.

When they reached the century the centurion in command asked, "Orders, my lord?"

"We are about to engage one of the enemy," Joran said. "It appears to be alone."

"Only one?" A legionnaire laughed. "Hardly need a full century for that."

"A similar creature infiltrated Tiber and killed over twenty city guards along with many citizens. That seemed to be a more advanced version, but you underestimate these things at your peril." Joran glanced around at the group. They seemed to be taking his warning seriously.

"Here's our plan," Mia said. "We're going to surround it, then use alchemist's fire to destroy it. Your job is to use your spears to hold it down and keep the fire from spreading."

"Can't we just use swords to carve it into pieces?" one of the men asked.

"These things appear resistant to normal weapons and their blood is highly toxic. A single drop on your skin would lead to instant death," Joran said. "For that reason, we deemed direct combat unwise."

"Understood, my lord," the centurion said, his bronze skin taking on a bit of a pale tinge.

A few bellowed orders got the soldiers in formation with Joran and Mia in the center. The group set out at a brisk march and an hour later reached a waiting scout. Without a word, the man pointed up the road where one of the zombies shuffled along, its black eyes fixed straight ahead. The creature wore the crimson and gold tunic of a member of the imperial army, though much like his melted skin, the uniform had seen better days.

"Centurion," Mia said. "Surround the target and hold it in place with your spears. We'll deploy the alchemist's fire when you're ready."

"Yes, ma'am."

A couple bellowed orders got the men moving and in less than a minute, they had the zombie surrounded. The creature seemed slightly confused, at least until an overeager soldier poked it in the chest with his spear.

The moment he did, some Black Bile oozed out and the zombie seemed to come awake. It grabbed the spear's haft just behind the head and jerked it hard.

The legionnaire foolishly tried to play tug of war with the monster and came out on the losing end. He staggered forward, finally abandoning his weapon a second before a crashing fist came down, missing him by inches.

As their comrade staggered back, a dozen soldiers lunged forward. They impaled the zombie from every direction and despite their numbers it still looked like they needed all they had to hold it in place. The creature's strength astonished Joran once again. The potential uses for such a powerful, tireless creature were endless.

Pity he had to destroy it.

He hurled an extra-large clay pot at the zombie's legs. The alchemist's fire exploded into flames that crawled up its uniform but had trouble consuming its flesh.

The zombie howled liked the damned thing it was and clawed at its flesh. Bile oozed out, suppressing the flames.

Joran hurled a second pot, this time hitting it in the chest.

The howling grew in volume and intensity as the flames roared to even greater heights. From his distant position, Joran grimaced at both the heat and the stink. Burning zombie smelled even worse than he'd feared, but at least the second vial seemed to overwhelm its defenses.

"Ware the trees!" a watching scout shouted.

Six more zombies burst out of the forest at a trot. This lot looked fully awake and ready for a fight. Even worse, Joran only brought two more vials of alchemist's fire, not nearly enough to deal with so many enemies.

"Withdraw!" Mia shouted. "Form up for a fighting retreat to the legion. Someone alert Her Majesty that we're incoming with enemies in close pursuit."

Her anxiety came through loud and clear through their link,

but Mia gave no outward sign of it. No doubt her training helped a great deal. For his part, Joran tried to focus on the still-burning zombie as they fell back. The flames had burned it down to a wriggling stump without arms or legs. Somehow what remained of its skull still howled.

He frowned. The others hadn't attacked until it started making that noise. Did the creatures have some sort of innate need to protect their own kind? He didn't know, but if they did, he had an idea that would making dealing with the rest of them much easier.

The retreat ended up being far shorter than Joran had feared. Alexandra showed up after only a quarter mile and the legion simply overwhelmed the half-dozen zombies with numbers and a river of alchemist's fire. It took almost no time for the new ones to start howling like the first. Lucky for them, there didn't appear to be any more of the vile things within hearing distance.

"That was more of an adventure than I'd hoped for," Mia said when the final zombie fell silent.

"It never occurred to me that they might come to each other's defense like that. It implies a level of awareness greater than they seemed to possess." He scratched his chin.

"What? I know that look, you're thinking deep thoughts."

"I don't know that, but as you spoke, I realized I *was* thinking too deeply. I gave the monsters credit for making a conscious decision to defend their fellows. What if, instead, their creator simply ordered them to attack anyone in the area when they heard that sound? It would be a simple way for them to spread out as far as possible and whenever one of them encountered someone and took a wound, the rest could charge in and tear apart whoever hurt the first one."

"How would you prove it either way and does it even matter?" Mia asked.

She had a point, but Joran hated questions with no answers.

"What kind of an incompetent idiot fails to notice a larger enemy force waiting in ambush?" Alexandra's enraged shouts drew Joran's attention away from his speculating.

One of the scouts had dismounted and she was currently dressing him down in front of the rest of the legion. The sight of the petite princess bellowing at a soldier twice her size who cowered in fear would've been comical if Joran didn't fear she might order him killed or whipped, or whatever punishment the legion dished out for scouts that failed to find a nearby enemy.

In this case, the scout hadn't actually screwed up and Joran hurried over before she got any angrier.

"Alexandra." When she turned her angry glare on him, Joran flinched. "It's not his fault. The zombies weren't that close and they had no reason to suspect otherwise."

"If they weren't that close," Alexandra said. "Then were the hell did they come from?"

Joran explained his theory. When he finished he added, "If I'm right, you can see how that might make our job easier."

She smiled her evil smile, seeming to have forgotten the scout for the moment. "I certainly can. Depending on how stupid they are, I can see a number of ways we might use this."

The scout caught Joran's eye from behind Alexandra and mouthed a silent, "Thank you."

"What do you say we find a good place to dig a pit?" Alexandra asked.

"I think that's an excellent idea. Then we'll just need some zombies to put in it."

———

The scouts, having overheard Alexandra giving the business to their fellow, worked extra hard to locate the bulk of the zombies. Just as Joran thought, they were spread out in a long, uneven line making their slow way north toward Tiber. One small piece of luck—the creatures hadn't encountered much in the way of civilization. Three destroyed farms and an abandoned village made up the bulk of the losses so far.

They hoped to eliminate the threat before any more people were killed. To that end, three centuries of troops labored to dig a pit forty feet across by thirty wide and twenty feet deep. That was the easy part of the plan. The hard part would be capturing a zombie without letting it make a sound until they were ready. Lucky for them, Joran now carried several adhesive vials with him at all times. The things were too useful not to have some on hand.

He'd given all but one vial to an elite squad chosen by Alexandra for exactly this sort of thing. For once, Joran didn't mind letting someone else take the risks. He and Mia had done their part and then some as far as he was concerned.

Besides, Alexandra forbade him to take any more chances. And if he didn't go, Mia couldn't either.

They had only an hour of daylight remaining when the filthy, exhausted soldiers climbed out of the pit. The workers retreated to the Second's camp leaving only Alexandra, Joran, Mia, and six centuries of infantry waiting for the capture team.

Happily, they didn't have long to wait. Less happily, two of the team came back draped over the backs of their horses. Dragged behind one of the horses by the ankles came a thoroughly gummed-up zombie. It wriggled around like a worm, silent and unable to attack.

"Prisoner captured, Majesty." The unit commander clapped his right fist to his heart. "What should we do with the ugly thing?"

"Toss it in the pit." Alexandra nodded toward the recently completed hole.

While four of the soldiers carried out her order Joran asked, "What happened to your comrades?"

The unit commander shook his head. "Damn thing moved faster than we expected. Beg pardon for the language, my lord. Before we got it bound, it killed two of my boys. Just bad luck. 'Soldier's luck' some call it."

"I've heard that expression, but it doesn't make the loss of a comrade any easier. Oh, and don't worry about offending me. Father used to take me to his warehouses when I was a boy. The teamsters can swear with the best of them."

The unit commander chuckled. "They can at that. Thank you, sir. I mean, my lord."

Joran clapped him on the shoulder and walked over to the edge of the pit.

Mia looked his way and shook her head. "It was kind of you to speak with him. Even a unit commander takes it hard when one of his people dies."

"Of course he does, he wouldn't be human otherwise. The way I see it, Alexandra can be the Iron Princess and I'll be the softie."

"The difference is, you aren't pretending." Mia tapped the side of her head. "I know."

By the time they joined Alexandra at the pit, the zombie had rolled about a third of the way across the bottom, which was plenty far enough.

"Ready?" he asked.

"Yes. I really hope this works." Alexandra glanced at him. "It will work, right?"

Joran held his hands out to the side, the solvent in his right hand. "In theory, but that's all it is until we test it."

So saying, he threw the vial, covering the thrashing zombie in greenish liquid. Instantly the adhesive started to break down.

"Let's go." Alexandra started back toward camp. "Hopefully in the morning we'll have a pit full of zombies."

CHAPTER 30

The Second Legion set up camp two hours north of the trap, far enough to avoid detection by any approaching zombies, but not too far. Or so Joran hoped. He'd been wrong about so many things, he no longer took anything for granted where these creatures were concerned. Still, they had to make some assumptions or they'd never take any actions.

He was busy trying to alleviate some of their ignorance. In a corner of the sprawling tent he shared with Mia and Alexandra, Joran had set up a tiny alchemy lab. Basically, his lab consisted of a table and the contents of his kit. Far from ideal, but in the field you had to make do, or so Mia assured him before she went to take a nap. Alexandra hadn't returned from inspecting the camp. Not that she doubted the soldiers, but a general had to do these things.

Joran just appreciated an hour to himself. He couldn't remember the last time he'd puttered in the lab, even a substandard one like this, trying to tease out the answer to a mystery. It felt good, like the days before his world turned upside down.

The mystery before him today was a sample of the black

ooze that served as the zombie's blood. He'd extracted a tiny sample from one of the legionnaires' spears and finally got to work. The first thing he learned surprised him the most. The substance wasn't actually Black Bile of the Earth. At least not pure Black Bile; a simple test confirmed that. But exactly how it had been altered and what the stuff did beyond kill a fraction more slowly than pure bile, he had yet to fully determine.

The fact that something had changed it in the first place came as a shock. He didn't think anything had the power to alter Black Bile. Certainly he'd never seen anything about it in any of the alchemy books he'd read at the college and he'd read most of them. The more strange things he encountered, the more a trip to the Forbidden Section of the library seemed unavoidable.

He grimaced and straightened, his back popping. Curious as he felt about whatever secrets the church kept hidden, drawing the attention of the Inquisition scared him more than fighting the giant serpent.

The tent flap parted and Alexandra strode in. Her expression immediately softened and she offered a lopsided smile. Her eyes were shadowed and not from the makeup she wore.

"How'd the inspection go?"

"Well enough, but I had to oversee the burial of those two legionnaires that died capturing the creature. I try my best to avoid those things, but when they act on your direct orders and end up dead, some responsibility settles on you. At least enough that you should attend their burial."

"If you'd said something, I would have joined you. I don't know if it would've helped, but at least you wouldn't have been alone."

She came over and rested her head on his arm. "Are you certain you're an imperial noble? You seem far too sweet."

"I am very much a reflection of those I deal with. Mia is the most important person in the world to me and will always be treated as such." Joran kissed the top of her head. "You are becoming more important to me all the time and if I've ever met anyone that needs to be treated sweetly more than you, I can't recall."

"You're an improvement over the generals, that's for sure. How's your project going?"

"Frustrating, but also fun. Unfortunately, I've about reached the limit of what I can accomplish out here. I've also reached the limit of my knowledge. Once we wrap up things here, I'm going to have to ask your father for permission to visit the Forbidden Section of the library."

"Father isn't going to want a fight with the church, but considering everything going on, it may be time to force the issue." She put her arms around him and Joran stroked her hair.

For a moment it felt like they were a real couple. They could pretend, at least for a few minutes, that over four thousand soldiers didn't surround them and just hold each other and enjoy the peace.

After a pleasant minute Alexandra looked up at him. "Having you here has enhanced my reputation. I've heard several people muttering about my new playthings. No doubt they have visions of us enjoying a nightly orgy."

"I dare you to tell Mia."

She laughed until a scream from outside brought their peaceful interlude to an abrupt end.

Mia came sprinting out of the side room where she'd been sleeping. "What's happening?"

"Good question." Alexandra stepped away from him and into the shoes of the Iron Princess. "Let's go see."

Joran had gotten so used to their near-constant presence that he hardly noticed the Iron Guard falling in around them. Two of them carried alchemical glow lights to push back the darkness. Outside, no one looked panicked, but the soldiers all had weapons ready to hand in case some enemy showed itself.

No more shouts rang out as they walked and soon enough Prefect Dantius came running up. "Majesty. The men. You have to see."

Joran and Alexandra shared a look.

"Get a hold of yourself, man." Alexandra looked like she wanted to slap him but held back. "Now what's all the fuss about?"

"Better if you see for yourself."

He led them to the edge of the camp and lying on the ground they found one freshly killed sentry and two bodies partially wrapped in dirt-covered uniforms. The dirty ones had been hacked into several pieces including having their heads brutally removed from their shoulders. The sentry's neck had been broken and his still-attached head hung at a grotesque angle.

"Those are the men you just buried, are they not?" Alexandra asked.

"Yes, Majesty," Dantius said. "According to the men that killed them, they dug themselves out and killed the sentry you see there before the others cut them down."

Alexandra immediately looked at him. "Joran?"

He knelt beside one of the severed heads. "Could I trouble one of you for a dagger?"

Mia handed him hers at once.

"Thank you." Joran cut the head's eyelids off and examined its eyes. They weren't the black pits he associated with the zombies, but they did have thin black lines running through them. "Looks like when the zombie killed them, some of its blood got in them. Not much, but enough to bring them back as a far weaker imitation of the original. From now on, we'll need to burn the bodies of anyone slain by a zombie."

Alexandra turned to Dantius. "See to it."

The prefect blanched. "The church says the dead must be buried."

"If the church has another way to keep the dead from rising,

I'll be happy to bury them. Until then, light the pyre."

"As *you* command," he said as if to emphasize that he was simply carrying out Alexandra's orders.

She nodded off to one side and when they'd moved a bit away said, "This didn't happen to the people that other one killed in Tiber."

"No, but she didn't kill them with her bare hands, remember? She used that black sword. Doubtless none of her blood got on them. That's my guess at least."

"Too many guesses, Joran. I'll speak to Father when we get back. If you need to get into the Forbidden Section, we'll get you there."

———

The next morning saw Joran, Mia, Alexandra, and a thousand members of the Second marching toward the pit they'd dug. The howling from the night before now emerged from multiple voices. From the sounds of it, Joran estimated they'd caught at least four or five of the zombies.

They approached with great caution, but nothing rushed out to attack them. Finally, they stood at the edge of the pit and peered down.

Joran had been underoptimistic. Seven zombies filled the pit, all of them moaning like the damned as if expecting more of their fellows to appear and fish them out. If more zombies hadn't shown up by now, Joran seriously doubted they'd be arriving at all.

"I'll be," Alexandra said. "It worked. Get the alchemist's fire and burn these things to ash. Dantius!"

"Yes, Majesty?" the prefect asked from six feet away.

"Divide the legion and get more of these pits dug in the creatures' path. Remind the capture teams to be extremely careful when they grab the bait."

"As you command. Where will you be?"

"I'm taking a thousand men and advancing to Fort Death. Most of the opposition should be well behind us when we arrive."

Dantius's throat worked as he tried to swallow, but at least he had sense enough not to question her orders.

It took the rest of the day for the group to march within sight of Fort Death. The sun had nearly set and it colored the stone bloodred, hardly an auspicious look. At least the walls and yard appeared silent and empty. As they'd hoped, the zombies had all vacated the area. Now they faced the prospect of either exploring the place now, or making camp and searching in the morning.

Joran cared for neither option, but Alexandra made the decision for him. "Break out the lights, we're going in."

The legionnaires went in first to confirm that nothing lurked in the shadows or outbuildings to threaten them. When they got the all-clear signal, Joran's group, surrounded by Iron Guards, entered the grounds. He couldn't deny that it felt far safer doing so with over a thousand armed soldiers than it had with the investigation team.

The keep door had been smashed to splinters. Joran sniffed and frowned. He'd expected the scent of Black Bile to be stronger now that the path to the basement had been opened, but if anything, only a faint whiff of the stench remained. His nose hairs didn't even burn.

Silence reigned inside the dark, empty keep. Joran raised his own blue light and a trio of guards added the golden glow of lanterns. Aside from a path that looked melted into the floor, no sign remained of what had happened.

"Where's the basement?" Alexandra asked.

Joran pointed and the group set out down the hall. A couple turns brought them to the access door. Even here the scent seemed mild.

They descended to the basement. Joran didn't even feel the need to dig out the protective face coverings they'd brought. The amount of miasma in the air simply didn't warrant it.

"Something's wrong," he said. "This close to the pool of bile we saw, the air should barely be breathable. This smells better than when it was sealed up."

"How is that possible?" Alexandra asked.

Joran shook his head. "I don't know, but there's one way to find out."

The group descended the ramp that led into the earth. The dark cavern appeared empty. Their lights reached from one end to the other, so nothing could be hiding. Whoever had spoken to them had fled, probably as soon as he sent his monsters out to kill them.

The pool of bile had vanished and where it sat only a circle of black metal remained.

"Does that metal look familiar?" Mia asked.

"Yes, it looks just like the sword we took from that woman." Joran stared at the few drops of bile remaining on the ground. He doubted enough remained to fill a vial. "Do you suppose that black disk covers a drain for the pool? And if so, where does it go?"

"I don't think I want to know," Mia said.

"You may not want to know, but we need to find out." Alexandra glared around at everyone and everything. "When we get back to Tiber, we're going straight to Father then you two will visit the Forbidden Section of the library. I don't care if the church doesn't like it, we need to know everything they're hiding."

Joran kept his mouth shut. Getting between the throne and the church terrified him in a way that nothing else had so far. If they weren't careful, The One True God cult wouldn't have to destroy the empire, it would tear itself apart from the inside.

EPILOGUE

The bitter northern wind slashed into Samaritan even with the protection of his alchemically treated cloak. In Tiber right now, it would be the middle of autumn, but here, winter had arrived in full force. An inch of snow covered the stone of the mountain pass he struggled to follow. The wretched weakness he'd been fighting since her death... He couldn't even think about it without the pain crushing his heart.

His dear soulmate. He wished more than anything to join her in death. And he would, riding a river of souls and screams as every citizen of the empire joined him. A fitting repayment for her murder. The thought of his, no, of *her* revenge, sustained him when the weakness threatened to overwhelm him.

He took a deep breath of glacial air and with it an infusion of ether. Some of the weakness washed away, enough to let him at least pretend to be a normal man for a few hours.

His cloak snapped under a particularly strong gust. It felt like another world up here after the heat of the jungle. With any luck he would have more success with his mission this time. If the ancient texts were right, the second weapon should be lying in wait under the mountains.

Perhaps it slept in a pool of lava like the serpent. The books didn't say. In fact, they were far too short on details for Samaritan's liking. Even worse, clearly the empire had become aware of his mission, or at least some of it. He would have to be especially alert for enemy forces. Especially his former comrades, the White Knights.

He pulled his cowl lower and tried to pick up the pace. The contact the archbishop promised should be around here somewhere.

Try as he might to focus, his mind kept drifting. Now it went to Antius and the mercenaries that killed *her*. Of all the people the pope might have sent, why did it have to be the one man he'd considered his friend in the order? He thought fondly of Antius. So earnest as a student and honorable as a knight. He held an unshakable faith, much like Samaritan had when he still thought of himself as Bellator.

But the world had a way of battering the faith out of you if you lived long enough. Maybe it was a mercy that Antius wouldn't make it that long. Beastmaster would see to that.

"Samaritan?" He had his sword drawn before he fully registered where the gruff voice came from. "The archbishop said you'd be along. Though she didn't mention you were so jumpy."

Samaritan finally spotted the owner of the voice. He—at least Samaritan assumed it was a he from the length of the beard—stood about four feet tall and wore a thick, fur-lined cloak and boots. The dwarf squinted at him through the wind.

"I am Samaritan." He sheathed his sword. "That makes you The One True God cultist that's supposed to guide me to the tunnels."

"Yup. Call me Grub. Let's get out of this God-cursed wind."

The dwarf stomped around a bend in the trail and vanished out of sight. Antius hurried to catch up. When he did, he found the entrance to a tunnel that ran deep into the earth. A crystal stuck in the rough stone wall burst into life when Grub touched it.

The tunnel seemed to go on forever, diving into the bowels of the earth. Samaritan would find the second weapon down there. And when he did, the empire would bleed.

AUTHOR NOTE

Hello everyone,

And so we've come to the end of Darkness in Tiber. The emperor my be saved, but the empire is still in serious danger. And that means Joran's life is only going to get more complicated from here on out.

I hope you'll join me next time when Joran, Mia, and Alexandra's adventure continues in Depths of Betrayal.

You can find links to all my books on my website, jamesewisher.com

Thanks for reading and I'll see you next time.

James

ALSO BY JAMES E WISHER

The Soul Bound Saga

An Unwelcome Journey

Darkness in Tiber

Depths of Betrayal

The Black Iron Empire

Overmage

The Divine Key Trilogy

Shadow Magic

For The Greater Good

The Divine Key Awakens

The Portal Wars Saga

The Hidden Tower

The Great Northern War

The Portal Thieves

The Master of Magic

The Chamber of Eternity

The Heart of Alchemy

The Sanguine Scroll

The Dragonspire Chronicles

The Black Egg

The Mysterious Coin

The Dragons' Graveyard

ABOUT THE AUTHOR

James E. Wisher is a writer of science fiction and fantasy novels. He's been writing since high school and reading everything he could get his hands on for as long as he can remember.

To learn more:
www.jamesewisher.com
james@jamesewisher.com

www.ingramcontent.com/pod-product-compliance
Lightning Source LLC
Chambersburg PA
CBHW020653030726
47498CB00002B/485